The Norman Conquest

A BOOK COMMEMORATING THE

Ninth Centenary
of the Battle of Hastings

COMPILED BY THE

Battle & District Historical Society

The Norman Conquest

ITS SETTING AND IMPACT

Professor DOROTHY WHITELOCK cbe

Professor DAVID C. DOUGLAS fba

Lieutenant-Colonel CHARLES H. LEMMON dso

Professor FRANK BARLOW d.phil.

EYRE & SPOTTISWOODE · LONDON

First published 1966
Reprinted 1966   1.2
Introduction © 1966 C.T. Chevallier
'The Anglo-Saxon Achievement' © 1966 Dorothy Whitelock
'William the Conqueror: Duke and King' © 1966 David C. Douglas
'The Campaign of 1066' © 1966 Charles H. Lemmon
'The Effects of the Norman Conquest' © 1966 Frank Barlow
Printed in Great Britain by
Richard Clay (The Chaucer Press) Ltd, Bungay, Suffolk

Contents

Illustrations

Acknowledgements are due for the following plates: to the Trustees of the British Museum and the Courtauld Institute for nos. 1 and 2*a*; to the Trustees of Winchester Museum and the Courtauld Institute for no. 2*b*; to Professor G. Zarnecki and the Courtauld Institute for no. 3; to the Phaidon Press and the Victoria and Albert Museum for nos. 4, 5*a* and 5*b*; to J. Manwaring Baines, FSA for nos. 6*a* and 6*b*; to Aerofilms and Aero Pictorial Ltd for no. 7; to the National Museum Record for no. 8.

Maps and Tables

The Norman Conquest

Introduction

by C. T. CHEVALLIER

The battle of Hastings was the last of those which have led to a conquest of England, and in the speed of its results the most decisive, for within five years the whole country was subdued by William; whereas the Roman conquest begun by Aulus Plautius took over thirty years to reach Carlisle; while, though the conquest of Britain by the English was altogether more penetrating and complete (for it imposed the basic English language and culture) yet it was effected piecemeal along the east and south coasts over fifty years and more, so that no single victory such as Hengest's at Crayford in 457 can be termed as decisive as William's at Hastings. As for the conquest by the Danes achieved under Sweyn and Cnut in 1013–16, this, by reason of previous settlements of Danes in eastern England since the days of Alfred, and of Cnut's moderation in governing more and more through Englishmen, had become by his death a successful merger rather than a conquest.

Readers of Colonel Lemmon's study of the campaign of 1066 will agree that the battle of Hastings was so closely and so long contested that, but for the depletion of the English forces through the losses sustained in routing Harald Hardrada near York on 25 September, and the resultant absence on the way south of more troops who would have turned the scale, William's brilliant invasion would probably have been defeated.

Naturally our French friends will find it hard to realize this, and will not be slow to recall that men of Normandy, Brittany and Picardy won the battle. We must accept this in good part, for so often the boot has been on the other foot. But we shall not because of this difference of viewpoint, or through any transitory divergences in the political field, refrain from welcoming the great French leader who continued his fight beside us from 1940 to 1945, if he will visit us on 14 October 1966. For we do not propose to celebrate what was a defeat of the English nation as it stood in 1066 – a compound of British, ex-Roman, Anglo-Saxon and Danish folk – but rather to commemorate the introduction of a fresh, able and virile element into our national personality – an element without which the nation must have developed on very different lines. Whether we like it or not, every single Englishman other than a recent immigrant must have Norman blood in his veins, mingled with English in thirty generations, for it has been estimated that by 1087 some 200,000 Normans and Frenchmen had settled in this country, while the native English population had fallen by perhaps 20 per cent to a million and a half.[1] From the known Norman combatants of 1066 hundreds of thousands can trace descent through female lines, not all through the aristocracy. Far more, it is understood, can do this in England than in France. Thus the present writer, of Jersey and therefore Norman extraction, can only show his descent from a Norman who fought at Hastings through the daughter of a minor Suffolk squire. To take a typical Englishman, Mr Harold Wilson presumably owes his Christian name to the revival of interest in King Harold as a national champion, brought about in the last century by E. A. Freeman and Bulwer Lytton; but undoubtedly he derives his surname from a medieval *Will* or *William*, a name which with-

[1] See J. Vising, *Anglo-Norman Language and Literature*, Oxford, 1923, p. 9.

out the Norman conquest would not be used in this country.

Therefore, although out of all the thousands who fought on Senlac ridge, we know the names of only some thirty Normans who both fought and later settled in this country (we know only eleven of the English), surely we can all in this centenary year join in praising famous men and our fathers on both sides, and commemorate the refounding of the English state which has evolved from the Norman conquest.

Certainly the townsfolk of Battle have cause to commemorate the battle on Senlac hill, for nothing in history is surer than that the high altar of Battle Abbey was erected before 1074 by King William's express order on the precise spot where King Harold fell. Behind it the new town grew up so vigorously on the previously bare ridge that within forty years of the battle the Abbey Chronicle[1] could include the oldest street directory in the country, giving in street order the names, occupations and rents (in pence and services) of 115 tenants of houses, all of whom 'on account of the very great dignity of the place are called BURGESSES'.

As part of the commemoration, the Battle and District Historical Society has invited three eminent professors and the society's president (a military expert in his own right, and the chief living authority on the battle fought in 1066) to contribute studies in the fields in which they are specially expert. They of course do not always agree among themselves – they have not been asked to – but they each lay before the public the fruits of many years' research. Where a work by one of them has been included in the bibliography, this has often been on the suggestion of another. This wide scope of their respective subjects calls for treatment in broad outline, with details included by way of illustration rather than controversy. The reader will

[1] British Museum MS Cott. Dom. A. ii. Translated M. A. Lower, *The Chronicle of Battle Abbey* (1066–c. 1190), London, 1851.

find no 'Freeman versus Round' polemics in these pages; but all four authors contribute from their several standpoints to our better understanding of the results which flowed from William's victory on Senlac Hill (*Santlache* as the Abbey Chronicle terms it) and his subsequent rapid conquest of this country.

Inevitably the four admirable studies could not cover all aspects of the story. Thus Professor Whitelock's brilliant survey of the Anglo-Saxon achievement over five centuries was not the appropriate setting in which to portray the details of Harold's career and background, in the manner so amply applied by Professor Douglas in the case of Normandy and William, or by Professor Barlow in his vivid analysis of subsequent developments. Nor indeed does sufficient material exist to support an essay on Harold on that scale. But to remedy this omission the committee has most kindly allowed me to add a few pages to this introduction. This will at least show the reader how sharply the work of an enterprising amateur falls short of the informed restraint of the professional historian; but also will convince him of the truth of the claim that in Battle we commemorate the vanquished as well as the victor. *Victrix causa deis placuit sed victa Catoni*; but we in offering this commemorative book to the public are at one with both the gods and Cato.

The Battle and District Historical Society accordingly presents this volume as an enduring means of commemorating the ninth centenary of the battle of Hastings, fought upon the site of the abbey and town of Battle.

The Background and Quality of King Harold

King Harold II, who was born about 1022 and fell in 1066, was not an upstart, as in some degree his father was. Godwine, who in 1018 suddenly became Cnut's earl of Wessex, was the only

Englishman given one of the four provinces into which the Danish king then intended to divide the country. But especially because Godwine gave his youngest son the name of Wulfnoth, it is reasonable to conclude that he was the Godwine to whom by his will the atheling Athelstan, Ethelred the Unready's eldest son, gave back the estate at Compton (probably the Compton near Chichester) 'which had been that of his father Wulfnoth'.[1]

The reference is most probably to 'Wulfnoth *Cild*, thegn of Sussex', who in 1009 when an accusation was laid against him by one Byrhtric made off with twenty ships from the new fleet which Ethelred had constructed at great cost to the whole country to oppose the Danes. Thus we find a most unworthy grandfather for Harold, one whose disloyalty was repeated in his grandson Tostig. The title *cild*, however, shows that he was of a distinguished family, presumably of the Sussex kingdom, probably banished when Offa conquered Sussex, but permitted much later to return; for we find a 'Wulfnoth thegn' witnessing the King Athelstan's charters regarding Sussex lands from 930 to 940, and another Wulfnoth selling Parham to the king's governor (prefectus) of Kent in the next reign.[2]

Probably during this exile from Sussex the Wulfnoth family settled in Kent. A marriage contract of 1017 was made between Godwine and the daughter of Byrhtric – clearly people of importance, for the witnesses included King Cnut and Archbishop Lifing. Thus it seems possible that this Godwine was the earl, though the name was common. Two Kentish Godwines are other witnesses, two more of that name and two Leofwines are among the sureties named for the rich gifts Godwine promised.[3] This may imply a reconciliation brought about

---

[1] D. Whitelock, *English Historical Documents*, Vol. 1, p. 550.

[2] See Dr Eric Barker, 'Sussex Anglo Saxon Charters' in *Sussex Archaeo-logical Collections*, Vols. 86, 87, 88.

[3] *English Historical Documents*, Vol. 1, p. 548.

B

English, Danish and Norman Dynasties

ETHELRED II 'The Unready' k. 978–1016
= (1) AelfFlaed

SWEYN 'Forkbeard' k. of Denmark. 986–1014 k. of England, 1014

RICHARD I, 3rd dk of Normandy, 942–996

RICHARD II 4th dk, 996–1026

Thorkils Sprakaleg

RICHARD III ROBERT I 5th dk, 1026–7 6th dk, 1027–35 = Herleve, who later = Herluin

Odo bishop of Bayeux, earl of Kent, 1067–82

Robert ct of Mortain

Athelstan EDMUND 'Ironside' k. d. 1016 d. 1015

(2) = Emma = CNUT the GREAT k. 1016–1035 = (1) Aelfgifu

Earl Estrith = Ulf

Gytha = Godwine Earl of Wessex

WILLIAM the CONQUEROR 7th dk, 1035–87 k. of England 1066–1087 = Matilda of Flanders

HARTHA-CNUT k. 1040–42

HAROLD I k. 1035–40

Alfred d. 1036

Sweyn II k. Denmark 1047–76

Beorn d. 1049

EDWARD the CONFESSOR = Edith Sweyn d. 1052 k. 1042–66

HAROLD II k. 1066

Tostig d. 1066

Gyrth d. 1066

Adela = Stephen ct of Blois

Edward Atheling d. 1057 (in England)

Goda = (1) Drogo ct of Vexin = (2) Eustace ct of Boulogne

Walter ct of Vexin, d. 1063

Leofwine d. 1066

Wulfnoth d. after 1087

Robert 8th dk 1087–1106

WILLIAM II 'Rufus' k. 1087–1100

Ralph earl of Hereford, d. 1057

Edgar Atheling d. c. 1125

Margaret = Malcolm III, k. of Scotland

Edith, renamed on marriage, Matilda = HENRY I k. 1100–35

STEPHEN k. 1135–54

NOTE: Queen Emma was probably not the eldest child of Duke Richard I, nor Queen Edith of Earl Godwine. Their names have been brought to the left to facilitate the tabling of their marriages.

by the king between the son of Wulfnoth and the Byrhtric who had vainly tried to overtake Wulfnoth in 1009. If so, the bride fetched to the Folkestone area from Brightling (near Battle) presumably soon died childless; for as a result of accompanying the king to Denmark in 1019 Godwine married Gytha, probably herself of Danish royal blood, a daughter of Cnut's first cousin and sister to Ulf who married the king's sister, Estrith. Gytha was the mother of Godwine's eight children, of whom the first four sons had Danish names. Harold, the second son, took his from Cnut's grandfather Harold 'Bluetooth' who claimed, rather prematurely, to have made the Danes Christian.

Godwine was for over thirty years the leading magnate under the English crown, though rivalled at times by one or other of the great earls. When Cnut died in 1035 Godwine supported his lawful heir by Emma of Normandy, Harthacnut; but as this prince, half Norman and half Dane, was absent in Denmark, most English magnates preferred Harold, Cnut's bastard son by a lady of Mercian family. It chanced that at a critical time in this dispute Alfred, Queen Emma's second son by her earlier marriage with King Ethelred, landed on a visit from his exile in Normandy – he had not seen his mother for twenty years. Godwine seized Alfred and handed him over to Harold's men, who blinded him so cruelly that he died soon after. Of this episode it can only be said that it was the sole crime laid at Godwine's door during his long career, in an age when noblemen were prone, not least in Normandy, to obtain their ends by such violence.

By 1042 both Harold I and Harthacnut were dead, and by popular acclaim Edward, Alfred's elder brother, was brought to the throne of his fathers after long exile in Normandy. Edward was never really reconciled to Godwine, even though he accepted him as the chief magnate and in 1045 took his daughter Edith to be his queen. Thus, when Godwine wished to use the newly restored fleet to aid the claims of his wife's nephew in Denmark, Edward supported the other magnates in refusing this. It was perhaps as a result of this that in 1050 the costly policy of maintaining a fleet was abandoned, and the makeshift alternative whereby London and the Kent and Sussex ports should provide ships when required, was substituted; an arrangement very satisfactory at the time to Godwine, because of his family ties with Kent and Sussex, but to prove a complete failure in 1066. Instead, a strong *élite* striking force of Housecarls[1] on the Danish model was re-established, ready to move rapidly to any scene of invasion, or itself to invade Wales.

When in 1051 Count Eustace of Boulogne was returning from a visit to Edward some twenty of his men were killed in an affray at Dover. Edward then ordered Godwine as earl of Wessex and Kent to go to Dover and sack the town. This Godwine with his Kentish background naturally refused to do; civil war threatened, and in the outcome the other magnates supported Edward in banishing Godwine and his sons; two of whom, Swegn and Harold, were already earls. The fall of the house of Godwine seemed complete, Godwine and his wife Gytha with their sons Swegn, Tostig and Gyrth went to Flanders, Harold and Leofwine to Ireland, Queen Edith was put in a nunnery. But within a year they were back in power; Harold had defeated the Devon and Somerset *fyrd* at Porlock, while Godwine had won over the ships and crews of Kent and Sussex, sailed up the Thames and overawed Edward's small fleet. The *status quo* before 1051 was restored by the Witan; thereafter until his death in 1053 Godwine was supreme, and after him his son Harold until 1066.

Fortunately the eldest son Swegn, against whom some

[1] For a description of the Housecarls see Colonel C. H. Lemmon's article, page 92.

outrageous acts were justly alleged, had died abroad in 1052. One of these was the murder in 1049 of his first cousin Beorn, who settled in England about 1044 and was given an English earldom. By 1047 Beorn's brother had become king of Denmark. Though the cause of the quarrel was a dispute about Swegn being restored to his estates by the king, Swegn may also have regarded Beorn's presence as a hindrance to his own position as a prospective leader of the Anglo-Danish element in England. Swegn invited him to Bosham in a friendly way, took him aboard ship, murdered him and deposited his body at Dartmouth. It was Harold who fetched the body for honourable interment at Winchester.

This, the first mention of Harold in the Anglo-Saxon Chronicle, shows him instinctively taking a course which he believed to be right, involving the honour of his house and the anger of his elder brother, and disregarding the risk. His success in the fight at Porlock and subsequent moderation presaged his successful campaigns and reconciling actions in Wales, and against Harald Hardrada in 1066, when after his victory at Stamford Bridge he allowed Prince Olof to return to Norway with twenty-four ships. Nothing adverse can be found in the Chronicle against him during the twelve years when, as minister and king, he governed England. His administration seems to have been characterized by steadfastness and consideration, and there is no suspicion of injustice or disloyalty. He had not the seemingly open and attractive disposition which made King Edward really fond of his brother Tostig. But when in 1065 Tostig proved unbearable as earl of Northumbria Harold, after striving for a reconciliation, accepted his inevitable banishment and the establishment as earl of Northumberland of the brother of his own nearest rival, the earl of Mercia.

When King Edward lay near death at the end of 1065 – he could not attend the consecration of Westminster Abbey on 28

December – leading members of his council were (in the opinion of our greatest living authority, Sir Frank Stenton) unanimous that Harold should be king. 'He succeeded to the kingdom as the king granted it to him and as he was chosen thereto' – so runs one version of the Anglo-Saxon Chronicle. Another version says that Edward on his deathbed 'entrusted the kingdom to the distinguished man Harold himself who the whole time had loyally served his lord, neglecting nothing that was necessary for the king of the nation'.

Of Godwine's other sons, Gyrth and Leofwine were for nine years earls, respectively of East Anglia, and of what we now term the Home Counties plus Kent, and fell fighting in the English counter attack, on Senlac hill.[1] But what of the youngest, Wulfnoth? We know on the authority of Eadmer that he was one of the prisoners released from custody in Normandy in 1087 under the Conqueror's deathbed orders. He is not named as escaping with his parents to Flanders or with Harold to Ireland in 1051. According to Norman sources, and also Eadmer, hostages were given on Godwine's return in 1052 for friendlier relations by Edward and Godwine, but it is unthinkable that in his hour of success Godwine would have allowed the dispatch of his son to Normandy. Presumably Wulfnoth (with his nephew Hakon, Swegn's son) was sent to William while Godwine was in exile early in 1052.

Whether Duke William came to England to receive a promise of the succession to the crown in this or any other period has been seriously doubted.[2] Very much more probably, a promise given by Edward before his own accession, was ratified in 1051 through Robert the Norman, then archbishop of Canterbury. As to Harold's oath in 1064 to support this promise, it may well

[1] See Colonel C. H. Lemmon's article, pp. 99 ff.
[2] D. C. Douglas, 'Edward the Confessor, Duke William of Normandy and the English Succession', *English Historical Review*, Vol. LXVIII, 1953.

seem inconsistent with Harold's character that he would have voluntarily made this oath, or that in his strong position at that time he would have accepted any instruction from Edward to go to Normandy to confirm William's succession. There is no record, except from the Norman side, that Edward ever gave him such an instruction; but a dominant motive for the journey can be found in Harold's loyal desire to recover his brother and nephew,[1] and his sanguine belief that, with Godwine long dead and after his own successful government of England for ten years, William would consider the situation entirely altered and would freely give up the hostages. Indeed he may have known little or nothing of what Archbishop Robert had negotiated in 1051. Suddenly confronted in Normandy with the sacred relics and required to swear an oath upon them, he could well have perceived that he was under duress, and that not only the hostages but his own liberty and even his life were at risk. So he swore the oath, and was allowed to return to England, with his nephew – but without his brother.

From the numerous children of his enduring union with Edith Swanneck no descendants can be traced, unless it could be from the marriage of a daughter into the Swedish–Russian aristocracy. His marriage *de convenance* with the sister of Earls Edwin and Morcar in 1065 produced no surviving heir.

A Note on the Bayeux Tapestry

As Professor Whitelock states,[2] this is English work, though being made under Norman direction it had to tell the tale its Norman patron wanted. Strictly it is a strip of embroidery, and

---

[1] This is the view taken by Eadmer, a monk of Canterbury, in his *Historia Novorum in Anglia*, written *c.* 1095. See G. Bosanquet's translation, *History of Recent Events in England* (London 1964), p. 6.

[2] See below, p. 41.

was clearly made by order of William's half-brother Odo bishop of Bayeux, for display in his cathedral which was consecrated in 1077. Odo's own part in council, campaign and battle is strongly emphasized, as would not have been the case had the strip been worked by Queen Matilda and her ladies in Normandy, as previously supposed. From the days of Edward the Elder the ladies of the English aristocracy were skilled in historical embroidery. The widow of Byrhtnoth who fell at Maldon in 991 presented such a hanging to Ely cathedral, illustrating her husband's noble deeds.

It is further most probable that this tapestry was worked at Canterbury, for the three insignificant personages depicted and named on it – Vital, Wadard and Thorold – were all retainers from the Bayeux area, who were given lands by Odo near Canterbury during the fifteen years when he was also earl of Kent.

Not only are Harold and other Englishmen depicted throughout with sympathy and respect, but, as American and German scholars[1] have pointed out, the purely English form for Hastings, AT HESTENGA CEASTRA, the crossed D, turning 'D' into 'th', and the dot over the Y in the name GÝRD, could only have been used by an Anglo-Saxon: 'Such purely English forms speak most strongly for the English origin of the tapestry.'[2] There was a good school of drawing at Canterbury.[3]

[1] Professors R. S. Loomis and Max Förster, cited by F. Wormald in *The Bayeux Tapestry* (ed. Sir Frank Stenton), 1957, p. 29.

[2] Max Förster, cited Wormald, op cit.

[3] Wormald, op cit., p. 34.

I · The Anglo-Saxon Achievement

by DOROTHY WHITELOCK

Elrington and Bosworth Professor of Anglo-Saxon
Cambridge University

In contrast to the Duchy of Normandy, which came into being as the result of a grant to Rollo in 911, the Anglo-Saxon state had had a long and by no means inglorious history behind it in 1066. Its people, who usually called themselves 'the English', had begun to settle in Britain about the middle of the fifth century, and by about a century later the settlements had coalesced into a few kingdoms, those south of the Humber often acknowledging a single overlord, a *Bretwalda* 'ruler of Britain'. Before the end of the seventh century all had accepted Christianity, and the sharing of a common church reinforced the sense of common origin, giving the members of the various kingdoms a feeling of unity. Thus St Boniface appeals in 738 to 'all God-fearing catholics in common, sprung from the stock and the race of the English', and Bede's pupil Cuthbert, a Northumbrian, wrote in 764 to Lul, a West Saxon, as was Boniface, his predecessor in the see of Mainz, saying that 'the whole race of the English, in whatever provinces they are found' should give thanks to God for granting Bede to their nation. When in the ninth century the Vikings menaced all western Europe, the courage and tenacity of King Alfred saved Wessex, and, though much of the north and east of England passed for a time under Scandinavian control, and received numbers of Scandinavian settlers, these areas were brought back under English rule by Alfred's efficient successors, his son Edward, his daughter Æthelflæd, his grand-sons, Athelstan, Edmund and Eadred. Athelstan was the first king who could claim to rule the whole of England; since he was recognized by some Celtic rulers, a charter refers to him as 'elevated by the right hand of the Almighty, which is Christ, to the throne of the whole kingdom of Britain'. He defeated at *Brunanburh* a great combine of Celts and Scandinavians, and he played some part in continental politics. Though there were short periods later when a Scandinavian king secured recognition in Northumbria, the last of these was killed in 954. Hence-forward, we have the united kingdom of England. The renewed Danish attacks in the reign of a weak king, Ethelred, resulted in the conquest by Cnut in 1016, but, contrary to what might have been expected, he reigned as his predecessors had done, upheld the laws and supported generously the church; those of his followers who were not already Christian seem to have con-formed. It is interesting to find, for example, a list of those who had entered into confraternity with the monks of Thorney Abbey, for the sake of their prayers, which begins with the names of Cnut's Danish earls, Turkil, Hacun, Eoric, Eglaf and his brother Ulf, followed by thirty-one Danish male names, presumably of their retinues. The English appear quickly to have civilized their Danish conquerors. The reigns of Cnut's sons were unpopular, but short, and in 1042 the English wel-comed back a king of their old royal line. A vernacular writer at Bury St Edmunds writes: 'May the noble name of our Lord the Saviour Christ be honoured for ever into eternity. . . . He in these days has given and granted the fair island of the kingdom of Britain to King Edward, just as He did of yore to his kinsmen.' By this time England had recovered its prosperity after the ravages of the Danish wars and the heavy tributes, and had become a rich prize to tempt the Norman duke.

During these six hundred years there were periods when the

Anglo-Saxon contribution to learning, literature and art had been spectacular. In the early eighth century Bede's writings showed him the foremost scholar of his age, in theology, chronology and history, and his work had a profound influence on the subsequent scholarship of all western Europe. His older contemporary, the West Saxon Aldhelm, was a man of great erudition, whose works continued to be used for centuries both at home and abroad. This period produced also masterpieces of manuscript illumination, sculpture and metal-work, and many manuscripts and works of art produced in England were taken to the Continent in the eighth century by the missionaries, Boniface, Willibrord and numbers of other Anglo-Saxons, men and women, who took the Christian faith to the heathen Germanic tribes. They established monasteries in Frisia and in the Rhineland, in which Anglo-Saxon learning and art flourished, and from which it spread to other foundations. Anglo-Saxon influence was not confined to these spheres, however, for St Boniface was instrumental in persuading the Frankish rulers to reform their church and to enter into closer relations with the papacy.

In the mid-eighth century continental students came to study at York, under Alcuin, an Englishman trained at the school of York established by Bede's pupil, Archbishop Egbert, and in 782 Alcuin went, at the invitation of Charles the Great, to play an important part in the Carolingian revival of learning, and by means of his pupils, some of them Englishmen, to influence continental scholarship of the next generation. Thus King Alfred had reason to remember with patriotic pride 'how men from abroad came hither to this land in search of knowledge and instruction'.

This period in which the Anglo-Saxons were influential on the Continent seems to have been the time when, at home, the bulk of surviving vernacular poetry was composed. This includes *Beowulf*, a rich and subtle poem in which a vivid account of the raids of monsters is told on a background of historical or heroic legend, with an underlying theme of the relation of monsters to a divinely created universe and of the qualities of a Christian hero and deliverer. There is also a deeply moving poem describing a vision in which the Cross tells its own experience at the Crucifixion, and brings home to the dreamer the full significance of the Christian doctrine of redemption; also some shorter lyric poems poignantly depicting tragic situations, such as that of a deserted woman, or of a man who has lost his lord, or lamenting the decay of earlier and greater civilizations, in order to conclude that the only true security lies in faith in God. There survives also a number of more directly religious poems, of various kinds, biblical paraphrase, homiletic and doctrinal instruction, saints' lives, etc. This early poetry was still being entered in manuscripts of the late tenth and early eleventh centuries. It is probable that poetry of this kind formed the inspiration of the Christian poetry of the continental Saxons, the *Heliand* and the *Genesis*. One of the leading missionaries to the Saxons on the Continent, the Frisian Liudger, was educated at York, where he would be likely to hear some Anglo-Saxon Christian poetry and to realize its value in teaching the faith to laymen.

King Alfred's reforms were directed to improve the state of learning in his own land, partly by the provision of English translations of Latin books 'most necessary for all men to know'. These remained influential in England; rather surprisingly, the Old English version of Orosius was taken to the Continent in the eleventh century, and was used there at a date when a familiarity with this language is unexpected. Yet it was not until the latter part of the tenth century, after a great monastic revival under the leadership of Dunstan, archbishop of Canterbury, Oswald, bishop of Worcester and archbishop of York, and Æthelwold, bishop of Winchester, that we get another great period of activity in learning, literature and art. From this time on, Anglo-Saxon manuscripts and works of art were again taken in numbers abroad, and proved influential in some continental houses. This 'golden age', which, oddly enough, was at its heyday in the troubled reign of Ethelred, differed from the 'age of Bede' in that one of its great glories was its vernacular prose, as we shall see later. During this same period, the Anglo-Saxons were exerting an influence outside their own land in another way: they played an important part in the conversion to Christianity of the Scandinavian lands.

There was certainly much in their past history of which Englishmen in the eleventh century could be proud, if they were aware of it. It may be of some interest to consider how far they were aware of history further back than living memory could take them. Educated men, not only ecclesiastics who knew Latin, but also laymen of the upper classes who read English, would be aware of the contents of Bede's *Ecclesiastical History of the English Nation*: its influence can be seen in later authors; manuscripts of the Latin text continued to be produced, while the Old English translation, probably commissioned by King Alfred, which was used by Abbot Ælfric about 990, survives in two tenth-century manuscripts and three of the eleventh century. The writer of an Ely charter in the early eleventh century cites as his authority 'Bede, the teacher of the English people', while a marginal reference, by the late tenth-century glossator, in the Lindisfarne Gospels to *Beda ðe bræma bæcere* ('the famous scholar') sounds like a quotation from a poem. Among the results of a knowledge of Bede would be the consciousness that they were descended 'from three very powerful nations of the Germans, the Angles, Saxons and

Jutes' and the belief that it was by special divine favour that their ancestors were allowed to conquer Britain. Pride in this conquest is shown in the final words of the poem on the battle of *Brunanburh*: 'the proud assailants, warriors eager for glory, overcame the Britons and won a country.' Bede's book also kept them aware of their debt to Rome, whence Gregory, 'Apostle of the English' had sent them the true faith. They were not to know that in 1066 the papacy would bless the banner of a foreign usurper.

Bede's history would take them only to 731, but there was also available the Anglo-Saxon Chronicle, which was first compiled from earlier sources about 890 and circulated to some religious houses, and thereafter continued in some places. A version which reached the north was interpolated with material taken from Bede and from sets of northern annals. Two of the three surviving versions which were being kept up in the reign of the Confessor were continuations of this northern recension; one of these, however, was by this time at St Augustine's, Canterbury, while the other, which betrays a special interest in the affairs of Northumbria and of the diocese of Worcester which was sometimes held in plurality with that of York, was probably at York (though some scholars would place it at Worcester). A third version, not based on the northern recension, was being written at Abingdon. These three versions are at times independent, and at other times two of them share a common source. There were other copies of the Chronicle which were not actively kept up, but which would be available for consultation on past history, and we learn of some lost copies; others may have been lost without trace. Thus many men would have an opportunity of reading about the Danish raids of the ninth century, about Alfred's victories and about the tenth-century re-conquest of the Danelaw. They could read also of the calamities of the reign of Ethelred, but the older men would remember these, and the younger know of them from their fathers' reminiscences.

An interest in various English saints helped to keep alive some knowledge of earlier history and customs. Manuscripts of early Latin saints' lives, Bede's *Life of Cuthbert* and the anonymous *Life*, Eddius's *Life of Wilfrid* (*c.* 709), Felix's *Life of Guthlac* (730–40), continued to be produced, as were also tenth-century works like Frithegod's *Life of Wilfrid* and Abbo's *Life of Edmund*, and the *Lives* of the monastic reformers, Dunstan, Oswald and Æthelwold. Felix's *Life of Guthlac* was translated into English, and there were several short vernacular *Lives* of English saints, some of them intended to be preached on their festivals. Many an illiterate Englishman would have learnt about some of these saints, though his knowledge might include later legendary material which had grown up round the cult.

Men of Latin culture continued to use the non-historical works of Bede, and the writings of Aldhelm (*c.* 686), whose difficult and ornate diction was often supplied with glosses in Old English, an indication that it was much studied. Manuscripts containing letters and poems by Alcuin were written in England in the eleventh century, and his works 'On Virtues and Vices' and the 'To Sigwulf on Genesis' were translated into English, the latter by Ælfric (*c.* 1000). The fact that most of the pre-Viking age English poetry has come down to us in four manuscripts written in the late tenth and early eleventh centuries may point to a deliberate attempt to preserve from oblivion their early literature.

Yet, as far as one can judge, most Englishmen of the eleventh century would know little or nothing about what to modern scholars is one of the greatest of Anglo-Saxon achievements, the work of the missionaries on the Continent in the eighth century, especially that of Boniface. Since he is not mentioned

C

by Bede or the Anglo-Saxon Chronicle, and since he was buried in Fulda in Germany and thus no English house could claim him as a wonder-working saint, little is heard of him in late English sources. No manuscript of any of the *Lives* of him appears to have been known in England, nor any of the collections of his correspondence and that of his successor Lul, which were made by their followers abroad. Only three of his letters can be shown to have been known in England at this time, and it was not interest in Boniface that preserved them. Two, in the original Latin, owe their preservation to the importance of their contents, for in one he and seven other missionary bishops attempted to persuade Æthelbald of Mercia to reform his ways, and in the other he sent decrees of a continental synod to Archbishop Cuthbert of Canterbury. A different type of interest led to the translation into English of a letter describing a vision of the next world seen by a monk of Wenlock, a type of literature which had a wide appeal. The scholar Archbishop Wulfstan II of York (1002–23) knew of some other eighth-century documents, but the average Englishman was probably quite unaware of this glorious period in his nation's past. Some who travelled abroad may have seen Anglo-Saxon manuscripts and treasures of the eighth century in continental houses; a far greater number of people would be aware that the productions in illumination, embroidery and metal-work of their own day were highly valued abroad.

Up till now, we have considered mainly what literate Englishmen in the Confessor's reign could read about past history. One must also reckon with oral tradition, which would reach far lower down the social scale. Some events may have been celebrated in poems, for it would be unwise to assume that the few historical poems which found their way into the Chronicle, and the single poem on a local hero, Byrhtnoth of Maldon, which a series of chances has preserved, are all which once existed: secular poetry had comparatively little chance of being written down. When King Ethelred's son Athelstan left to his brother Edmund in his will in 1015 'the sword which King Offa owned', we can well believe that he knew far more about this great eighth-century king than he could have learnt from the scanty entries in the Chronicle; the great dyke stood as a tangible memory of Offa's power and efficiency. Abbot Ælfric was probably not drawing on written sources alone when he selected as kings to compare with the Emperor Theodosius as being 'victorious through God', Alfred 'who often fought against the Danes, until he won the victory and protected his people', Athelstan 'who fought against Olaf and slew his army and put him himself to flight' and Edgar 'who exalted the praise of God everywhere among his people, the strongest of all kings over the English nation', for whom 'God subdued his adversaries, kings and earls, so that they came to him without any fighting, desiring peace'. Though not all the stories which reached the early twelfth-century historian William of Malmesbury are acceptable as history, there is no reason to disbelieve his claim that the places where Alfred suffered ill-fortune were still being pointed out by the local people. There must have survived a widespread admiration for Alfred as a man who snatched victory when in an apparently desperate position; otherwise we should not find two religious houses in the early eleventh century eager to secure the credit for their own saint: Durham attributed the victory to the help of St Cuthbert; St Neots claimed it for their saint, and in the vernacular *Life of St Neot* occurs the earliest recorded version of the story of the cakes, told to emphasize the depths of misfortune from which the saint rescued the king. Alfred lived on in popular memory also as the writer of books: when Ælfric speaks of the 'books which King Alfred wisely translated' he probably knew which these were, but the words of his contemporary, the chronicler Æthelweard, 'an unknown number of books', and those in the *Life of St Neot*, 'he composed many books through God's spirit', suggest a vaguer tradition. Middle English poetry shows that long after the Norman conquest the memory survived of Alfred as 'the wisest man that was in England'. Stories concerning Athelstan also reached William of Malmesbury; and as for Edgar, traditions concerning his care for justice, his organizing of the fleet and his reform of the coinage were eventually written down by post-Conquest writers.

We are therefore probably justified in believing that many people in Edward the Confessor's time were fully conscious that their nation had produced strong and victorious kings, and learned and saintly men; and they thought of their nation as a unity, in spite of local variations in customs and institutions. They would be unlikely to welcome the prospect of a ruler from an upstart state across the Channel; they would not consider their civilization and government inferior to that of Normandy, nor, as we shall see, had they any reason to do so.

It is hardly necessary nowadays to go to great trouble to refute earlier charges of decadence or incompetence levelled against the Anglo-Saxons of the eleventh century, for studies of surviving records and objects have already shed a favourable light on many aspects of their culture, and continue to do so. It is enough to let the facts speak for themselves. In the course of a long history, the monarchy had acquired greater powers than those possessed by most rulers in western Europe, and the kings in the tenth century, who were faced with the task of ruling the whole of England, had established a measure of uniformity in certain large matters, while permitting local differences in institutions and customs, especially between the Danelaw and the rest of England. The division into shires, which was ancient in Wessex, was extended over the whole country as far as the Tees, the shire-meeting being held twice a year. The division into hundreds, which may also have been ancient in some parts of the country, was spread everywhere, except in some Danelaw areas, where the functions of the hundred were performed by a district known as a weapon-take; the hundred ordinance of the mid-tenth century secured uniformity in administration. Its court met every four weeks. Its duties included the maintenance of order by taking action against cattle-thieving, by ensuring that every man had sureties capable of bringing him to court, and by its jurisdiction over all but the gravest criminal suits. The hundred court also apportioned the incidence of taxation. There were also borough courts, which met three times a year, and we hear of courts where two or more hundreds were combined, while in the north there was a court of the riding. The shire court dealt with both criminal causes and civil causes concerning land, and it is in connexion with the latter that documents survive which supply us with vivid glimpses of the thegns of the shire settling local disputes. It is interesting to see how often they prefer to bring the parties to some measure of agreement rather than enforce the letter of the law. Typical is the statement in an account of a Worcestershire lawsuit between a certain Leofric of Blackwell and a man called Wulfstan: 'Then both Leofric's friends and Wulfstan's said that it would be better for them to come to an agreement than to keep up any quarrel between them.' Though many details of the working of the various courts are obscure, there is enough to show that there was an efficient system of local government in force, and this impression is supported by the insistence of the Norman kings that it should in essentials remain unchanged. Again and again we find them referring questions to the shire or the hundred, and a writ of Henry I in 1108 declares that the shire court and the hundred court are to be held in the same places and at the same fixed periods as they were held in the time of King Edward, and not otherwise. Though most suits were dealt with at these local assemblies, it was the king's justice they administered. The hundred was normally presided over by a king's reeve, the shire by the ealdorman or the sheriff, along with the bishop in suits which concerned the church. The increasing tendency in the later Saxon period for the ealdorman to be in charge of several shires led to greater responsibility of the sheriff for his own shire; but both ealdorman and sheriff were royal officials, and in addition, the king might sometimes send a special messenger to the meeting. There were some hundreds in private hands, which meant that the representative of the holder of the privilege presided, and that the profits of jurisdiction went to the latter; but these immunities were always derived from a royal grant. Moreover, there were certain serious criminal charges which were almost always reserved to the king, and not included in a grant of privilege, namely breach of the king's protection, forcible entry into a house, ambush, the harbouring of fugitives and the fine for neglect of military service. Only a very few highly privileged persons were allowed to handle these.

The law which the courts administered was a mass of customary law with various local differences, but supplemented and modified by the statutes of successive kings; for kings in England had been for centuries accustomed to legislate, and codes survive from seventh-century kings of Kent, from Ine of Wessex (688–94), from Alfred and from most of his successors up to Cnut. The laws of Offa of Mercia, which were known to King Alfred, have not survived. Archbishop Wulfstan II, who held the province of York 1002–23, speaks many times with admiration of the laws of Edgar, and made great use of the code which we cite as II and III Edgar when drafting several codes for King Ethelred and a comprehensive code for Cnut. This was the last Anglo-Saxon law-code, and when King Edward in 1065 had to yield to the Northumbrians in revolt against their earl, Tostig, we are told: 'and he renewed there the law of King Cnut.' When documents of the Norman kings insist on the observance of the laws of King Edward's time, they mean this code and established custom, and Cnut's laws are given the place of honour by the Latin writers who in the reign of Henry I translated and made compilations of the Anglo-Saxon codes and wrote treatises of the law. This was not done in a purely antiquarian spirit, for only a few changes had been introduced by William I, e.g. the murder-fine to protect his Norman followers, the use of the ordeal of battle as an alternative to the Anglo-Saxon methods, and a sharper differentiation between ecclesiastical and lay courts. The continued respect paid to Anglo-Saxon law is strikingly illustrated by the bringing of the aged bishop Æthelric of Selsey to the plea held on Pinnendon Heath in 1075 or 1076 in order to answer questions on Anglo-Saxon law. The two most comprehensive manuscripts of the Anglo-Saxon laws were compiled in Henry's reign, namely the *Textus Roffensis* and the St Pauls manuscript now in Corpus Christi College, Cambridge.

If William was content to make few alterations in the law, he also had little reason to be discontented with the royal rights held by his predecessors. Besides the profits of jurisdiction, the king had over the whole land the three public dues, fortress work, bridge work and military service. From these, immunity was hardly ever granted. Though the precise details of the amount of military service which could be demanded are uncertain, and seem to have varied in some places in accordance with individual agreements made with the king, there is no doubt that his rights were extensive. The Anglo-Saxon military organization was adequate to preserve the land reasonably secure from the Welsh and the Scots, and at Stamford Bridge a great army led by the foremost Scandinavian warrior of the time was utterly defeated. Even after the Norman kings had made arrangements for a feudal army, by granting estates to be held by knight-service, they still continued on occasions to call out the native levy.

The king possessed extensive royal lands in most parts of his kingdom, and they could be increased by the forfeiture of lands for grave offences, and by the royal right of inheritance after foreigners or others who died without heir. He had widespread rights to tolls, and from many estates he still received food-rents, relics from a time when this charge had been incumbent on all lands, though by the eleventh century the granting of land by charter, as 'bookland', which was freed from this payment, had greatly decreased the area which paid it. It was probably in relation to these food-rents and to military service that the country was first assessed in hides (in some Danelaw areas in carucates); but by the late Saxon period this assessment was mainly important for the collection of the geld.

This tax, one of the main sources of royal income, had originated from the need to buy off Viking invaders, but was later used to pay a standing army or navy, and eventually to meet any special need. To operate it, an efficient and flexible system had been evolved by which the geld was taken at a rate per hide which could be varied according to needs, and a sum was demanded from each shire according to the number of hides it was assumed to contain; this sum was then divided among the hundreds of the shire, and eventually among the estates in the hundred in relation to their assessment in hides. The collection of this tax, and the handling of the royal revenue from all its varied sources, imply an expert and centralized financial system in advance of its day; the Norman kings used it with little modification for a long period. They also inherited an excellent coinage: beside the Anglo-Saxon silver pennies the coins of the duchy of Normandy before 1066 make a poor show. From the eighth century onwards the high quality of Anglo-Saxon coins caused them to have influence on the Continent, and in the eleventh century a coinage on the English model was introduced into Scandinavia. A firm central control was kept; by the end of the period dies were cut at London, and circulated to the local mints, of which in Edward's reign there were about seventy; new issues were made at regular intervals, and the money paid by the moneyers for the new dies went into the royal coffers. A few ecclesiastics, e.g. the two archbishops and the bishops of Hereford and Rochester, were allowed their own moneyers. The fact that coins of Harold's brief reign survive from more than half of the known mints is evidence for the speed and efficiency with which the system worked. William took it over in full working order.

There was thus a high measure of centralized government, and its successful working was made possible by what Sir Frank Stenton has called 'the most efficient means of publishing the ruler's will which western Europe has so far known', that is the 'writ', a simple letter in the native language, authenticated by the king's seal, which gave instructions regarding the king's wishes or information regarding his acts. Numbers of these writs have survived, usually addressed to the bishop, earl, sheriff and thegns of the shire, or to the bishop, town-reeve and citizens of the borough. A casual reference in a late tenth-century homily, 'If the king sends his writ to any one of his thegns', suggests that it was common for the king to communicate by this means with individuals, but naturally the writs which had most chance of surviving were those which a religious house had an interest in preserving, those which made grants to them or re-established their claims to estates or privileges. For these purposes the writ began to supersede the older formal Latin 'diploma' as evidence of such rights, though diplomas of the old type could still be drawn up occasionally, even after the Conquest. The Norman kings took over the writ in order to communicate with their subjects for all manner of administrative purposes, though gradually it came to be written in Latin and supplied with a short list of witnesses. One writ of special interest just after the Conquest is not a royal one, but written in the name of the Confessor's widow, Edith, sister of King Harold: it is addressed to the hundred of Wedmore, informing it of a grant to the canons of Wells, which is the reason for its preservation; but in addition it asks 'that you will pronounce for me a just judgement concerning Wudumann to whom I entrusted by horse(s) and who has for six years withheld my rent'. No doubt numbers of writs dealing solely with ephemeral matters of this nature have perished without trace.

The powers of an Anglo-Saxon king were considerable, though during the later Saxon period the increasing tendency to combine several shires under a single ealdorman, or earl, as he was universally called by Edward's reign, gave this official more influence than had previously been the case. The politics of this reign were disturbed by the rivalry between the families of Earl Godwine and Earl Leofwine. Yet the notion of a hereditary earldom had not got very far. In principle, the earl was the king's nominee: Archbishop Wulfstan's statement, 'a thegn becomes entitled to an earldom by the king's gift', was copied in a manuscript about the time of the Conquest. In practice, something like a hereditary right of the house of Leofric to the earldom of the original Mercia seems to have been acknowledged, but this did not prevent small earldoms from being carved out of the great area which had formed the Mercian kingdom, and these were given to men of other families. For example, Swegn, Godwine's son, held the Mercian shires of

Gloucester, Hereford and Oxford along with the West Saxon shires of Berkshire and Somerset, and on his death Hereford and Oxford, at any rate, were given to the king's half-Norman nephew, Ralf. An earldom in the East Midlands was held along with Northumbria by Siward, and then it passed to Tostig, Godwine's son, in whose time it can be shown to include Huntingdonshire, Northamptonshire and Bedfordshire. It was only after Tostig's expulsion that it was given to Siward's son Waltheof. Godwine was earl of Wessex and Kent, and earldoms were created for his sons as they grew up: Swegn held the one already mentioned, Harold had East Anglia until he succeeded his father to Wessex, Tostig was appointed to Northumbria in 1055, Gyrth was given East Anglia when Ælfgar, Earl Leofric's son, who had succeeded Harold in this area, became earl of Mercia after his father, and Oxfordshire also was added to Gyrth's earldom, and finally, Leofwine, Godwine's son, held Essex, Hertfordshire, Middlesex and Buckinghamshire along with Kent and Surrey. Harold combined Herefordshire with his earldom of Wessex. The complicated re-arrangement of earldoms during this reign looks like deliberate policy: it would not weaken the house of Godwine as long as members of this held so many earldoms, but it would prevent the establishment of earldoms with settled boundaries in which sons might claim to succeed their fathers by right, instead of by royal gift. Without unduly minimizing the power of Godwine and his sons, especially after their triumphant return from exile in 1052, we should note that this return was made possible in part by the wish of both sides to avoid serious civil war. As the Anglo-Saxon Chronicle says: 'It was hateful to almost all of them to fight against men of their own race . . . and also they did not wish the country to be laid the more open to foreigners through their destroying each other.' Even after Godwine's victorious return, the king was no mere cipher, completely controlled by a powerful subject: loyalist attachment to the house of Alfred was strong, and, as we have seen, many institutions made the power of a central government felt throughout the country, mighty though the local earl might be.

Though powerful men, Osgod Clapa in 1049, Godwine and his sons in 1052, Earl Ælfgar in 1055 and 1058, Tostig in 1066, did not shrink from using armed force to recover their position after they had been exiled, the rivalries between comital families did not go as far as private warfare, and there was no need in England to establish a 'truce of God' as was done in Normandy to prevent private warfare during certain periods. Naturally, England was not free from deeds of violence. Northumbria in particular was a wild land, and we read of a long feud between two local families, in which the part played by a certain Thurbrand in the slaying of Earl Uhtred in 1016 was avenged by Uhtred's son Aldred, who then in his turn was killed by Thurbrand's son Carle; the last act in this drama was the slaughter by Aldred's grandson Earl Waltheof of most of Carle's sons in 1073. Yet this does not seem to have involved others than the families concerned, and in any case the north was exceptional. The Northumbrians who rose against Tostig in 1065 did great damage round Northampton while waiting for the king's reply: 'they killed people and burned houses and corn and took all the cattle that they could get at . . . and captured many hundreds of people and took them north with them, so that that shire and other neighbouring shires were the worse for it for many years.' Individual acts of treachery and cruelty are occasionally recorded, such as the blinding of the atheling Alfred in 1035, and Earl Swegn's murder of his cousin Beorn in 1049. Similar incidents can be found in all countries at this time, and perhaps what one should notice is how both these actions shocked contemporary English opinion: they were not taken as normal. Judged on eleventh-century standards, Anglo-

Saxon England must have appeared a comparatively peaceful place. The readiness of local thegns to settle disputes by compromise no doubt is one element in the comparative freedom from private conflicts. One gets the impression from the documents that the country was rich in good sense.

Without internal peace, England would not have recovered so rapidly from the devastations of the Danish wars. Its wealth is not disputed, and the bulk of surviving coinage implies a considerable amount of trade. Already in the reign of Ethelred we learn that English ships were to be expected in continental harbours, and English traders in Rome, while a document from about this time refers to the presence in London of traders from Normandy, Ponthieu, Flanders, Lorraine, France and the territories of the emperor. There was also considerable trade with Scandinavia, especially from York and the eastern ports, and Bristol and Chester handled trade with Ireland; one gets a casual reference to Irish traders with cloaks to sell in Cambridge. The imports seem mainly to have been luxury goods, wine, spices and incense, precious metals, gems, ivory and silk, rich robes, furs, glass vessels and some types of pottery; oil and blubberfish are mentioned also. We learn less about exports. Fine embroidery and metal-work of English manufacture were prized on the Continent, but the chief exports were probably wool and agricultural produce, especially cheese. The fact that these things could be produced in excess of home needs suggests that in some areas at least the land was being competently farmed according to eleventh-century standards. Both the law and the church forbade the sale across the sea of Christian men; yet some traffic of slaves to Ireland was carried on at Bristol as late as the reign of William I. The slave class was probably shrinking before the Conquest because of the frequency of manumission by the owners as a charitable act for the good of their souls. Manumission continued after the Conquest, and gradually the clear distinction between a slave and a free man of the lower classes on economically much the same level became blurred, since the Norman lords judged more by tenurial dependence than by the possession of a wergild (the price to be paid in compensation if a man were slain), which was in Anglo-Saxon times the mark of a freeman.

The increase in trade had been accompanied by an extension of urban life. This had received encouragement from the policy of Alfred and his son Edward the Elder of building fortified boroughs as a defence against the Danes, for these offered security as trading centres. It became increasingly common for landowners to possess at least one house in neighbouring boroughs, while important magnates, ecclesiastical or lay, usually had property in many large towns, and especially in London. Most citizens were regarded as tenants of the king, and in general he retained the main share of rents, services and profits of jurisdiction, though in many boroughs the earl had a third of the profits, and in some, as at York and Worcester, the archbishop or bishop owned part of the borough; it was common also for landowners with houses in a borough to have the right of jurisdiction over their own men occupying them. Boroughs were in charge of a town-reeve, and there was a borough court which King Edgar ordered to meet three times a year. It is not possible to access accurately the population of Anglo-Saxon towns, since Domesday Book gives only the number of messuages and we do not know how big an average of inhabitants one should allow to each. London and Winchester are not described in Domesday Book; York seems to have had some 1,800 messuages, Norwich 1,320, Lincoln 1,510, while several other towns, e.g. Chester, Oxford, Hereford, Gloucester, Worcester, Thetford, Ipswich, etc, though smaller, were by no means negligible. After the Conquest, and partly as a result of it, trade increased and with it the size of towns; but not uniformly nor immediately: Domesday Book reveals a decay in some towns between 1066 and 1086.

Criticism of the eleventh-century Anglo-Saxon church nowadays comes mainly from those who judge a church by its monastic fervour. The zeal of the reformers of the tenth century, which had led to the displacement of secular canons by monks in some places, and to the foundation or re-foundation of many Benedictine monasteries, had largely spent itself by the eleventh century, and the only sizable Benedictine houses to be founded then were Burton-on-Trent about 1004, and Bury St Edmunds, founded by Cnut in 1020, though there were also smaller foundations. An attempt was made in the laws of King Ethelred to insist on a communal dormitory and refectory in churches served by bodies of canons, and, though this did not become universal, some prelates of Edward's reign, such as Archbishop Ælfric at Beverley and Bishop Giso at Wells, imposed it. New foundations in this reign tended to be for bodies of canons, as were Stow, Lincolnshire, founded in the early eleventh century, and later endowed by Earl Leofric, and Waltham Holy Cross, enriched by Earl Harold, and the smaller foundations of Axminster and Cirencester. Throughout the period people also continued to be generous in gifts to the older establishments, in lands, money and ornaments. Lay donors include the earls, Siward, Ralf, Odda, Leofric, Tostig and Harold; and of particular interest are the many grants made by landowners to parish churches. Individual piety showed itself also in the prevalence of pilgrimages, to Rome and even to Jerusalem.

It became common in the eleventh century for bishoprics to be given to the king's priests, men who had served him in his writing office, whereas before the episcopate had had a preponderance of monks. This method of rewarding ecclesiastics who had carried on the essential civil service was not confined to England, nor does it follow that the king's priests who were thus advanced (and by no means all of them were) were unsuited for the episcopal office. Contemporary criticism seems levelled at only two of them, Ulf, a Norman whom Edward made bishop of Dorchester, and who would have been deprived at the Council of Vercelli (1050) if he had not had recourse to bribery (or so the Anglo-Saxon chronicler believed) and Stigand, a grasping prelate who held sees and abbacies in plurality, even after becoming archbishop of Canterbury. Most of the bishops appointed from among the king's priests appear to have given satisfaction, and not only as administrators. Leofric of Exeter collected books and enriched his church with them and with artistic treasures, as well as with land. On the other hand, when the choice fell upon a monk, as it not infrequently did, some of these proved active men of affairs. It is true that the reign of the Confessor produced no one of the stature of Archbishop Wulfstan II of York (1002–23), who combined deep scholarship with political and administrative ability, and carried out reforms in many aspects of religion, the effects of which reached far beyond his diocese, but the episcopate in 1066 included St Wulfstan of Worcester, a man of piety who was regarded as an ideal bishop, and Aldred of York, an outstanding administrator and political figure. Few appointments seem to have been made without good reason, though in England as elsewhere there was some danger of influence and simony. However, the English church did not appoint to sees mere youths related to the reigning house, as was sometimes done in the duchy of Normandy.

What is of particular interest in regard to the late Anglo-Saxon church is the amount of evidence showing a deep concern with the religious needs of the laity and with the condition

1. 'Christ entering Jerusalem' from a psalter of about 1050

2a. The Godwine Seal
in the British Museum,
dated about 1000.
Found at Wallingford,
Berks.

2b. An ivory of about
1000 in Winchester
Museum

of the parish priests in charge of them. A large number of homilies were produced, especially by Ælfric, abbot of Eynsham, to be preached by the clergy to bring home to ordinary men the central doctrines of the faith, to preserve them from heresy, and to inculcate proper Christian behaviour. Ælfric issued between 990 and 991 two volumes of homilies for the major festivals of the Christian year, and during the rest of his life he continued to revise these, and to add new homilies for Sundays not covered in his original work, as well as a series mainly of lives of saints, which might urge men to emulation of their virtues. From the manuscripts of these works which survive, it is clear that they were much used and copied. His contemporary, Archbishop Wulfstan II, also wrote many homilies, some of straightforward instruction on doctrine and morals, some of impassioned appeal for repentance. These too became widely known. Both these writers also produced works in Latin and in English which are directed towards the improvement of the secular clergy: Ælfric wrote for these pastoral letters, at the request of Bishop Wulfsige of Sherborne and of Archbishop Wulfstan, who himself is the author of sets of canons. One of Wulfstan's most interesting writings is a little tract on the need for more careful instruction and examination of candidates for orders. This is a practical document, and while it admits that there might be occasions when out of necessity one would have to ordain a 'half-trained' candidate, it insists that such a man must give an undertaking to continue his studies. Both Wulfstan and Ælfric, monks by training, make many appeals for a celibate priesthood, but with little obvious success; Wulfstan seems to have had to tolerate married priests in his northern diocese. His writings also consider the duties of bishops and of bodies of secular canons; there seems in fact no section of the church which he does not examine. Though after his death in 1023 the Anglo-Saxon

D

church produced no one to equal him, a continued interest in these reforms is shown by the production of manuscripts of his work, as well as of Ælfric's, and of translations of canonical writings of continental authors. There is no reason to suppose that the average bishop neglected the spiritual needs of his diocese; care for these is not incompatible with vigilance over the temporal possessions of their church, though the nature of our surviving records makes this appear to loom more largely.

Latin scholarship had flourished after the tenth-century monastic revival, as is proved by saints' lives and canons written in this language, by the continued production throughout the period of manuscripts of Latin authors, and by the wide knowledge of these visible in the works of men like Ælfric and Wulfstan, who were familiar with many works of the Fathers and of Bede, Aldhelm and Alcuin, as well as with canonical writers, especially of the eighth and ninth centuries. For the teaching of Latin, Ælfric composed a Latin–English grammar, and an amusing colloquy to exercise his pupils in Latin vocabulary. Yet the glory of the late Anglo-Saxon period was its English writing. At a time when no vernacular prose of any distinction had appeared on the Continent, the Anglo-Saxons had developed a language of great copiousness and flexibility, capable of rendering Latin works on theology, philosophy and science. They had translated the gospels, most of the first seven books of the Old Testament, the Benedictine Rule and that of Chrodogang of Metz, some of Alcuin's treatises, and of the canonical writings of Amalarius of Metz and Theodulf of Orleans, and some of Bede's scientific work. These translations show a great advance in style on the renderings in Alfred's reign of Gregory's *Pastoral Care* and *Dialogues*, Augustine's *Soliloquies*, Boethius's *Consolation of Philosophy*, Bede's *Ecclesiastical History* and Orosius's *History against the Pagans*, which were still available. Many of Ælfric's homilies are based on Latin sources, but not slavishly; they show a control of language, a grace and a balance, which has never been surpassed. A different, but still a distinguished style was written by Wulfstan, capable of eloquence and force, and there are other excellent varieties of style in various anonymous authors. Strong and vivid narrative, not dependent on Latin originals, is found in the Anglo-Saxon Chronicle. Though the reign of Edward produced no writers of the calibre of Ælfric or Wulfstan, and though one can rarely date anonymous prose, the Chronicle and some charters show that the power to write good English prose not only continued until 1066, but survived in some places as late as the early twelfth century. But the copious vocabulary needed for abstruse subjects did not survive, since after the Conquest Latin was used for such themes. A distinguished foreign scholar has commented: 'It is almost pathetic to ponder on the expenditure of energy that was literally wasted, and the unrealised endeavour swept away by political change, through no inherent deficiency of its own.'[1]

No good Anglo-Saxon poetry later than the poem on the battle of Maldon, composed not long after the event of 991, has survived; the few later poems in the Chronicle and some didactic religious verse are of very inferior quality. As has been mentioned above, the chances of survival of secular poetry of the Maldon type are poor, and hence we cannot be sure that this poem was the swan-song in which the heroic ideals of loyalty and courage, of preferring death to flight, found their final expression. Yet one may feel that the ideals themselves were not dead, and that the stand made by some of Harold's followers after his death at Hastings would have lent itself to a similar treatment to that given to Byrhtnoth's bodyguard

[1] Otakar Vočadlo, 'Anglo-Saxon Terminology', *Studies in English*, iv, Prague, 1933.

at Maldon: 'Here lies our lord, all cut down, the hero in the dust. Long may he mourn who thinks now to turn from the battle-play.' What, however, we do know is that Anglo-Saxon poetry in the alliterative metre must have survived underground, to emerge again, with modifications, in Middle English in Lagamon's *Brut* and in the fourteenth-century alliterative poetry of the West Midlands.

The Benedictine revival of the late tenth century resulted in a great flowering of manuscript illumination, which owed much to continental models, but soon branched out in independence. It produced two main types: fully painted miniatures and pictures, often in a framework of acanthus-leaf design, in rich colours and gold; and outline drawing of great vivacity, characterized by delicacy of line and a remarkable power of imaginative suggestion. There survive a number of fine manuscripts from the last hundred years of Anglo-Saxon rule, mainly psalters, gospels, benedictionals and other books of ecclesiastical use, though there are others: the *Psychomachia* of Prudentius was often illustrated, and there is an illustrated copy of Gregory's Commentary on *Ezechiel*, one of Aratus's astronomical work, the *Phænomena*, one of Ælfric's *Heptateuch* and one of the Junius manuscript of Old English religious poetry in the Bodleian Library. Several illuminated manuscripts produced in England were taken abroad. Our records tell us of some donors, for example that Cnut and his wife Emma gave a sacramentary and a psalter to Cologne, that Emma gave a benedictional to Robert, abbot of Jumièges and that an abbot of Ramsey gave illuminated manuscripts to Fleury. But even without such references, surviving manuscripts would show the export of English illuminated manuscripts to the Continent, and their influence can be seen in the products of some continental houses, such as St Bertin's at St Omer and St Vaast at

Arras. In the latest pre-Conquest examples of English illumination, some of the earlier freedom and spontaneity has given way before an urge to stylization and pattern, but it remains an expressive and beautiful art. In some English houses, at least, its influence continued after 1066, all the more easily because the Normans had been familiar at home with the styles based on the Anglo-Saxon manuscripts which they had imported. Plate I reproduces one of many beautiful outline drawings contained in a psalter of about 1050.

Artistic products in other media had less chance of survival: objects in precious metal tended to be melted down in times of stringency, and textiles and wood are perishable materials. The richness of Anglo-Saxon England in works of art in these materials can be learnt mainly from references in our sources, in narratives, in wills and lists of benefactions, and in inventories, often of later date. We learn of crucifixes and images in, or covered with gold and silver, sometimes studded with precious stones, of valuable church plate and candelabra, of magnificent vestments, banners and tapestries: we read that 'English work' in precious metal and in textiles was valued abroad. The quality of English embroidery can be seen in the remarkable stole, made between 909 and 916, which was found in St Cuthbert's coffin, and the post-Conquest Bayeux tapestry is English work. Ivories also survive, and some smaller objects of metal, to show the artistry and skill of Anglo-Saxon craftsmen. Plates 2a and b illustrate two ivory objects of the late tenth or early eleventh century. As for stone-carving, the date of some of the finest examples is disputed, but most experts now assign to the late Saxon period such dignified sculptures as the Langford and Romsey roods and the Barnack 'Christ in Majesty' (Plate 3).

No just appraisal of late Anglo-Saxon architecture can be made, seeing that none of the cathedrals or larger monastic churches have survived. It would appear, however, that even ambitious prelates had not been inspired to emulate the grandiose churches which were springing up on the Continent, and, as far as we know, that only Edward the Confessor's church at Westminster was built in the new fashion. The Anglo-Saxons seem to have been loath to sweep away earlier buildings long hallowed by religious use, and in some places the need for greater accommodation was met by the adding of a new church on the axis of one or more older churches. At St Augustine's, Canterbury, Abbot Wulfric planned to join two earlier churches by means of a great rotunda, but the Conquest intervened, and it was never completed. We have to judge, therefore, from the smaller churches. Far more Anglo-Saxon work survives in our parish churches than has hitherto been realized, and records show that several were being built right at the end of the period. We read, for example, of churches consecrated by Wulfstan, bishop of Worcester, 1062–95. Among the more impressive examples of late Anglo-Saxon architecture are the churches of Stow, Lincolnshire; Worth, Sussex; Hadstock, Essex; St Benet's in Cambridge; and the well-known towers of Earl's Barton and Barnack, Northamptonshire, and Barton-on-Humber, Lincolnshire, which afford good examples of the decoration by means of pilaster-strips, arcading and long-and-short work at the quoins, and of the double belfry windows, characteristic of this period.

It has not been the intention of this chapter to demonstrate how much of the civilization of the Anglo-Saxons survived the Norman conquest; this has been touched on here and there, when it was necessary to use post-Conquest evidence to prove that some aspect of this civilization was still vigorous in 1066. The Normans made many changes: a new aristocracy replaced the English higher classes, mainly holding its lands by knight service, and one result of this was to lessen the freedom with which women could hold land; the higher ecclesiastical offices were filled by Normans, and this brought the English church more rapidly into contact with continental developments in scholarship than would otherwise have happened; for a time Latin largely superseded English for official purposes, and Norman French as the spoken language of the upper classes. Yet, in the end, it was English, reinforced with much vocabulary from French, which conquered. William established a stronger monarchy than that of the Anglo-Saxon kings, but in doing so he was building on the foundations which these had laid. Yet, even if the Conquest had been as destructive of what went before as used once to be believed, the six centuries of Anglo-Saxon rule in England would remain a remarkable achievement.

II · William the Conqueror : Duke and King

by DAVID C. DOUGLAS

Emeritus Professor of History, University of Bristol

This book is designed to commemorate the nine-hundredth anniversary of the battle of Hastings. The battle is described in detail and its consequences are to be considered both in relation to the ancient English kingdom which was thereby to pass under a new ruler, and in connexion with the political and ecclesiastical changes which thereafter ensued. The other papers in this volume thus deal with large questions of general importance to English history, with which the present essay has no concern. But there may be room in such a commemoration for a comment on the personality and career of the central figure in the drama of 1066 – the Norman duke who on the evening of 14 October 1066 stood victor on the downs above Hastings, and who, on the next Christmas Day, was hallowed as king of the English in the abbey church of St Peter at Westminster.

But even if the subject be thus rigidly circumscribed, it none the less presents difficulties. So much has been written on William the Conqueror that it might well be doubted whether anything more could usefully be said about him. He is familiar to schoolboys and scholars; facts and fictions about him are part of the currency of general conversation; and even to-day he is one of the few figures in the English story about whom it is considered shameful, or eccentric, to profess ignorance. The fact, indeed, deserves some note. England is perhaps unique among the nations in having taken so thoroughly to herself a successful invader from overseas; and she has been content to start the long succession of her numbered kings from a man who began his rule by conquest.

Considering the remote age in which he lived, and the circumstances of his life, it is surely remarkable that this eleventh-century magnate of foreign birth should have entered so deeply into the English consciousness. That he has done so might of itself be cited as testimony to his historical importance. But it has been due also to the fact that the literature concerning him has been not only of long duration but of a very peculiar character. A mass of erudition has been expended upon his life and work; and over the centuries a war of words has raged about him. His career has provided a constant text for political controversies and social sermons, to such an extent that sometimes he has almost seemed to remain a figure in contemporary politics. He has been presented in terms of Whig theory, of sectarian fervour, and of modern nationalism. He has been hailed as one of the founders of British greatness and as the cause of one of the most lamentable of English, defeats. He has been pictured as an enemy of Protestantism and as both the author and the subverter of the English constitution. Indeed, it might almost be said that the influence which he has exercised on English growth has been conditioned not only by what he did but also by what men thought, or imagined, or hoped, that he did.

Even to-day, it is hard to escape from the consequences of these controversies, but it is clear that any description of the Conqueror, and any account of his life, must seek to do so. William, if it be possible, must be pictured against his own eleventh-century background. More particularly must he be placed in his own Norman setting. Not only was he a Norman by birth, but the major part of his life was spent in Normandy.

It was as a Norman duke that he came to England, and his conquest was effected by one who had already shown himself the exceptional ruler of an exceptional province. And it was as a Norman king of the English that (for good or ill) he influenced the subsequent development of England. His career did not begin in 1066 nor did it then end, and it will be a primary purpose of this essay to suggest that what he accomplished as king must be closely related to what he had earlier achieved as duke.

William the Conqueror was born in 1027 or 1028, being the bastard son of Robert I, sixth duke of Normandy, by Herleve, a girl of Falaise, and on his father's death in 1035, he became, when still a child, the ruler of a province which was then unique in Christendom. Normandy in 1035 can be regarded as the product of two contrasted traditions, both of which were to affect the whole career of William himself. The first was Scandinavian. It is very usual to ascribe the special characteristics of Normandy to the intrusion of a Scandinavian population into this region of Gaul during the previous century, and to find the starting-point of the history of medieval Normandy in the establishment of Rolf the Viking (Rollo) and his followers in Neustria between 911 and 918 by means of grants made by the Emperor Charles III. Nor is evidence wanting to support such an interpretation. Later chroniclers assert that there was a considerable repopulation of Neustria in the tenth century, and it would seem that the flourishing ecclesiastical life which had formerly distinguished the province of Rouen was severely disrupted by the invaders. The surviving lists of Norman bishops show gaps at this time which are testimony to the disintegration that had occurred, and it is probable that in the third decade of the tenth century not a single monastery remained in the Norman land. Again, despite the politic conversion of Rollo to Christianity, the ruling dynasty itself seems only slowly to have renounced the traditions of its Viking past. Even as late as 996, a French chronicler could refer to the Norman duke as a 'pirate chief', and within twenty-five years of the birth of William the Conqueror his grandfather welcomed in his capital of Rouen a Viking host which had recently spread devastation over a considerable area of north-western France. In short, it would be rash indeed to minimize the Scandinavian factor in the making of the Normandy which William ruled.

On the other hand, it would be equally rash to give it too great a prominence. On many of the great estates of Normandy the events of the tenth century do not seem to have interrupted a tenurial continuity which apparently here proceeded with scarcely more modification than elsewhere in Gaul, and the place-names of Normandy have been held to indicate a society in which men from the north formed only a minority. These, moreover, seem soon to have been absorbed. Adémar of Chabannes, writing about 1030, goes out of his way to emphasize how quickly the new settlers had adapted themselves to the civilization into which they had entered, and we have the contemporary word of Dudo of Saint-Quentin that by 1025 Scandinavian speech was already obsolete in Rouen though it still persisted in Bayeux. At the same time, trade and ideas flowed across the insubstantial land boundaries of Normandy and up and down the great waterway of the Seine. Viking Normandy, in fact, quickly assimilated the surrounding culture of France, and despite the survival of Scandinavian traditions among them, William and his followers when they came to England were French in their speech, in the essentials of their culture and in their political ideas. It was in keeping with the earlier history of Normandy that one of the chief results of the Norman conquest was to deflect the destinies of medieval

England away from the Scandinavian north and towards Latin Europe.

William's reign as duke of Normandy was also to be conditioned by the fact that the province over which he presided was itself of ancient delimitation. It was in fact almost precisely the pre-Viking ecclesiastical province of Rouen with its six dependent bishoprics, and this in turn was based upon a division of the old Roman Empire. The ducal ancestors of William had thus been able to build upon established foundations, and they had in fact used many of the older institutions of government, inheriting traditional rights to revenue and to military obligations, inheriting, too, such powers as had been vested in the counts of the Carolingian age, and also authority over constituted local officials such as the *vicomtes*. This was, in fact, to stand William in good stead during his terrible minority, and it helps to explain his survival during the perils of his early years. His succession as a bastard child in 1035 tested the ducal authority to the uttermost, and the horrors of his boyhood have been often and luridly described. His court was a shambles; his guardians nearly all perished by murder; and he had himself frequently to be taken from his home by night to seek refuge in neighbouring dwellings. Elsewhere the province was given over to private wars among the greater Norman families, almost all of whom were involved at this time in violence or disaster. There is no doubt that William's minority was one of the darkest periods in Norman history.

That these calamities were not (as might have been expected) fatal to William, and to Normandy, was certainly due in part to the inherited authority that had come to be vested in the ducal office. It is remarkable, for instance, that during these tumultuous years nearly all the *vicomtes* regularly discharged their duties; the ducal revenues continued to be collected; and the bishops of Normandy seem, in general, to have given their support to the child ruler. It would appear also that the boy duke, or those who acted for him, had a specifically ducal force at their disposal. In short, the traditions of ducal authority and the administrative machinery which might give it effect were sufficiently strong to enable the ducal power to survive the critical decade between 1035 and 1046. How important this was can be judged by reference to the revolt of the western *vicomtes* which broke out in 1047, when the duke needed to be rescued by his overlord, the French king. By that time, however, William had reached maturity, and was beginning to exercise his personal influence on the afflicted duchy he had inherited.

Yet if the battle of Val-ès-Dunes signalized the end of Duke William's minority, it marked also the beginning of six more years of uninterrupted war in his struggle for survival. It is unlikely for instance that the strong fortress of Brionne in central Normandy held by his enemy Guy 'of Burgundy' was retaken before the end of 1049, and it is doubtful whether William was able to re-enter his capital of Rouen before 1050. At the same time Geoffrey Martel, count of Anjou, who had risen to a position of dominance in western France was starting to exercise pressure on Normandy through Maine. As a result, during the winter of 1051–2 Duke William was engaged in his famous campaign which resulted in the sack of Alençon after siege, and in the capture of Domfront. In all this continuous warfare between 1046 and 1052 it should be noted, moreover, that William had the support, active or passive, of King Henry of France. But before 15 August in the latter year Henry transferred his support from the Norman duke to the count of Anjou, and henceforth the king of France, far from being the ally of Duke William, was always to be his most formidable opponent in Gaul. This transformation of political filiations has been described by a great French historian as constituting nothing less than 'a turning point in history', and certainly its

3. 'Christ in Majesty', Barnack, Northants

AROLD:SACRAMENTVM:FECIT:✣ hIⵏ
VVILLELMO DVCI:✣

4. 'Harold's oath before William' from *The Bayeux Tapestry*, edited by Sir Frank Stenton (Phaidon Press)

results were to be far-reaching. The relations between Normandy, Anjou and the Capetian monarchy were to be affected for more than a century with consequences that were not to be fulfilled until after 1154 when Henry II from Anjou became duke of Normandy and king of England.

These were long-term developments, but the immediate effect of the change was to create a lethal threat to Duke William whose danger was further enhanced by the fact that it was not only from outside Normandy that he was now menaced. During these same months, two of his uncles, William, count of Arques and Mauger, archbishop of Rouen, who between them controlled much of eastern Normandy, revolted against their young nephew. William, therefore, once again faced destruction, for there is little doubt that if this coalition from Arques and Rouen, from Anjou and Paris had ever been brought in unison against him, he must have succumbed. In the event, he was able to capture the stronghold of Arques before Normandy, early in 1054, was invaded by a strong force collected from all over France by the French king. It entered Normandy in two sections, and the main contingent was heavily defeated in February 1054 at the battle of Mortemer. It was an important engagement, for at Mortemer the crisis of Duke William's Norman reign was met and passed, and never again was the integrity of his duchy to be threatened as it had been imperilled between 1046 and 1054. The French king's raid in 1057 which was repelled at Varaville was a minor affair, and the deaths of Geoffrey of Anjou and King Henry of France in 1060 did but give final assurance that the perils which had been faced during the previous fourteen years had at last been surmounted.

The severity of the long struggle which occupied all the youth and early manhood of William the Conqueror needs to be borne in mind in estimating his character and assessing his

E

achievement. Indeed, one of the most difficult questions of Anglo-Norman history is here involved. In 1066 William was able to effect the conquest of a great kingdom. But it is by no means easy to explain how he was able to undertake such an enterprise, and still less easy to explain how he was able to bring it to a successful conclusion. In 1054, when he was at last freed from his worst perils, he was some twenty-six years of age; all his life, he had been involved in defensive war; and Mortemer is separated by only twelve years from Hastings. The contrast between the strength of Normandy in 1066 and its weakness at the beginning of William's reign is in fact so remarkable that it is only to be explained firstly by the personality of this young ruler, and secondly by reference to aristocratic and ecclesiastical developments within Normandy which William somehow succeeded in harnessing to his own policy and his own purpose.

It is unnecessary to emphasize the importance to William's achievement of those great Norman families whose names were to become household words in medieval England, and indeed in medieval Europe. This was perhaps the most remarkable secular aristocracy produced in Europe during the earlier Middle Ages, so that it is important to note that it was in 1066 only of comparatively recent establishment. Few, if any, of these families can be traced back before the first quarter of the eleventh century, and many of the greatest of them such as Tosny, Beaumont, Grandmesnil and Montgomery only then acquired their landed wealth, and the territorial names by which they later came to be distinguished. Their advance was, however, thereafter to be extremely rapid, and it presented special problems for Duke William. It is thus of fundamental importance to an explanation of William's later achievement that under his rule as duke the rise of this aristocracy should have been made to contribute not to the disunity of his duchy but to its strength.

For this was not inevitable. Feudal organization developed gradually in Normandy with the tumultuous rise of this new nobility: it was not imposed, as in England, by the administrative policy of a prince. All the more notable, therefore, was it that William managed to enlist the support of these families to his own cause during his hazardous reign as duke. His success in this must be attributed to his own personality. Already in 1051 during the campaign round Domfront we find closely associated with the duke a group of young men (*tirones*) which included William fitz Osbern (later earl of Hereford) William I of Warenne (later earl of Surrey) and Roger II of Montgomery (later earl of Shrewsbury). Again, during the defence of Normandy against the French king in 1054 the war was waged by families who were in each case operating near their own estates: Tosny, for instance, in central Normandy; Mortemer and Giffard in the east. The result was notable; and it was to affect all the future. After the defeat of William, count of Arques, in 1053, there was no major revolt among the Norman aristocracy, and in 1066 the vast majority of the Norman nobility were ready to stake all their newly-won fortunes on the success of Duke William's adventure overseas.

Equally important to the development of Normandy under Duke William was an ecclesiastical revival. This, particularly in respect of the Norman monasteries, has attracted so much attention from historians that there is little need to comment upon it further. But it is important to note that this movement, also, was of comparative late development. The first definite evidence that the Norman bishoprics were being reconstituted comes from a charter of 990, and of the ten principal religious houses that were in existence in Normandy at the time of William's accession only four had been re-established before

1000, and four more had been set up since his birth. The subsequent resuscitation of Norman monastic life was, however, to be astonishingly rapid, and after 1047, the new Norman aristocracy took over from the ducal house the work of patronage; so that by 1066 the Norman land was famed throughout western Europe for the extent and for the quality of its monastic life. Distinct from this, but by no means negligible, was the work of the Norman bishops between 1035 and 1066. Their achievements were in the main – though not exclusively – mundane. Hugh, bishop of Lisieux, and John, bishop of Avranches, were by any standards notable prelates, and the history of Normandy and England would have been very different apart from the careers of Odo, bishop of Bayeux, and Geoffrey, bishop of Coutances. The general result of this ecclesiastical revival was to prove little short of spectacular. An ecclesiastical province, of no abnormal size, which in 1066 could be represented by men of such contrasted distinction as Odo of Bayeux and Geoffrey of Coutances, Maurilius, archbishop of Rouen, John of Avranches, Hugh of Lisieux, Lanfranc, then abbot of St Stephen's, Caen, John, abbot of Fécamp, Herluin, abbot of Le Bec, and the young St Anselm, was in very truth not to be ignored.

The ecclesiastical and aristocratic developments in Normandy during Duke William's Norman reign were, throughout, most closely associated both with each other and with the policy of the duke. The new aristocracy had shared with the duke the sponsorship of the monastic revival, and, with the single exception of Maurilius, archbishop of Rouen, from 1054 to 1067, all the Norman bishops of this time were members either of the ducal house or of the greater Norman families. In this way the aristocratic, the ecclesiastical and the ducal advance in Normandy had become merged into a single political achievement which could perhaps be summarized by saying that in 1065 a man might go from end to end of Normandy without ever passing out of the jurisdiction, secular or ecclesiastical, of a small group of inter-related great families with the duke at their head.

For William had established himself at the centre of this progress. He had identified with his own, the aims of the new aristocracy. In like manner, his influence pervaded the reformed Norman church being expressed in all major appointments, and more particularly in the provincial church councils. But perhaps this inter-related development was expressed most clearly in his ducal courts, which, attended by the secular and ecclesiastical magnates of Normandy, steadily increased in importance after 1054. It was in every way a notable *curia* which, sometime after 1060, confirmed at Bayeux the gifts made by Bishop Odo to his cathedral church, and equally notable was the court which, early in 1066, ratified at Fécamp grants made to the abbey of Coulombes. Most certainly, too, the assembly which met at Caen in July 1066, and which, as stated in the relevant charter, looked out on the comet which was even then illuminating the Norman skies, was a court of which any European ruler might have been proud. It symbolized the rapid and intense concentration of power which had been accomplished in this province of Gaul, and which was itself one of the most notable political phenomena of mid-eleventh-century Europe. From this, indeed, was to derive much of the strength which made possible the improbable success of William's invasion of England.

William's invasion of England was not only facilitated by the developing strength of the province he ruled. It was the outcome of a policy which was of long duration. The establishment of the English Danelaw, and of the Viking dynasty in Neustria had forged links between England and Normandy from which neither could escape. The momentous marriage in 1002 of Ethelred II to the daughter of a Norman duke had given dynastic expression to this inter-dependence, and the deposition of Ethelred, and Emma's second marriage to Cnut, his supplanter, was of scarcely less importance to Normandy than to England. Nor was it merely the ruling families which were concerned. The political filiations of England with Scandinavia, and the changing position of Normandy within Gaul, were likewise reciprocally involved. Yet if William was, here, heir to a tradition he, none the less, enlarged it. Even during his boyhood the issues that were involved were being given clearer definition. He may well, for instance, have watched the exiled sons of Ethelred II at his father's court. The athelings, Edward and Alfred, took refuge in Normandy very shortly after the establishment of Cnut in England, and their claims to England were kept alive in the duchy. It was during this period for instance that Edward's sister Goda was given in marriage to Dreux, count of the Vexin, who was the ally of the Norman duke; and William of Jumièges, who is usually to be relied upon, asserts that William's father actually planned an invasion of England on Edward's behalf and collected ships for that purpose. The story is unconfirmed, and, though not impossible, must be received with caution. But there can be no doubt that Edward's succession to the English throne in 1042 could be regarded as in some sense a victory for Norman policy. The murder of his brother Alfred in England in 1036 had caused an outburst of indignation in Normandy, and it was to be used at a later date as a cardinal point in Norman propaganda which made Godwine, earl of Wessex, responsible for the crime. Certainly, after Edward's accession, the Norman dynasty, under William, must have felt itself in some measure committed to the cause of the new king in England.

It will be recalled also how conscious Edward the Confessor

was of this, and how ready he was to turn to Norman support both in his dealings with the great earls of Northumbria, Mercia and Wessex, and in the hazardous defence of his kingdom against Scandinavian attack. But certain qualifications should be made with regard to his acts in this respect. His policy of introducing Normans into England was not wholly original, for some Normans had followed Emma to England in 1002, and, though these receded into the background after her marriage with Cnut, they were precursors of the men who responded to her son's invitation. Moreover, the new Norman aristocracy was, during these years, too fully occupied in establishing itself at home to pay much attention to England. Indeed, of the laymen who came from France to England in this period few, except Earl Ralph the Timid from the Vexin (the son of Dreux and Goda) were of the first rank, and no Norman layman at this time seems to have been given possessions in England of any wide extent. In the church, however, the situation was different. Norman clerks appear in the royal household early in Edward's reign, and the introduction of Norman prelates into England such as Ulf, bishop of Dorchester, William, bishop of London, and more particularly Robert, abbot of Jumièges who became archbishop of Canterbury in 1051, was a characteristic feature of the reign. Nor is there much doubt that, as generally believed, Edward had by 1051 designated Duke William as his heir.

In these circumstances, the unsuccessful rebellion of Earl Godwine in 1051, his triumphant return in 1052 and the succession of Harold to the earldom of Wessex in 1053, were obviously of direct concern to Normandy since these earls of Wessex were irrevocably opposed to the Norman succession in England. But between 1051 and 1054 Duke William could make no intervention in English affairs, since, as has been seen, he was during those years involved in one of the major crises of his own reign. Nor was he able to oppose the plan formulated in England during the next four years to substitute as the Confessor's heir, the Atheling Edward (son of Edmund Ironside), who was then an exile in Hungary. After the atheling's return from exile, and his very suspicious death in England in 1057, the Norman duke must surely have realized that his chief opponent in England was likely to be Harold Godwineson who, from this time forward, was evidently contemplating the succession for himself. All the complex elements in Anglo-Norman relations thus began to be crystallized into an individual rivalry between two of the most remarkable personalities of eleventh-century Europe.

But William must also have been aware that the impending struggle would be a triangular contest. It was as well known to him as it is to us that England had recently formed part of a great Scandinavian empire, and that there were Scandinavian princes whose claims were pressing and exigent. Indeed, the threat to Edward himself from this quarter had been persistent. It is permissible to surmise that, in 1047, only the death of Magnus of Norway had prevented an invasion of England which might well have been successful, and in 1058 the son of Harald Hardrada, king of Norway, attacked England with a large fleet collected from the Hebrides and from Dublin. The attempt failed in its purpose, but it clearly foreshadowed the greater expedition which Harald Hardrada was himself to launch in 1066. William's policy towards England was thus always bound to take account of Scandinavia.

Before 1066 it had, moreover, been given further precision not only by the developing strength of Normandy (which we have watched) but also by the duke's changing position in the political structure of Gaul. In 1050 or shortly afterwards William made his famous marriage with Matilda daughter of Baldwin V count of Flanders. The lady was it seems of diminutive size, but she appears none the less to have been one of the few persons who were not overawed by her formidable husband, and on occasion she could act as regent for him. William on his part is stated to have been notoriously devoted to her so that she may have had some personal influence on his career. But it was the political implications of this match which were from the first important. The marriage took place despite papal prohibition (allegedly on grounds of consanguinity), and for this reason William's relations with the papacy were to be strained for nearly a decade, until in 1059 Pope Alexander II sanctioned the marriage, and William and his wife in return undertook to build the two great monasteries in Caen which to-day commemorate them so worthily in stone. In 1050, however, the marriage was chiefly significant as indicating the place which the young duke was beginning to win for himself among the greater fedatories of north-western Europe, and in fact the Flemish alliance was to persist until after the Norman conquest of England which it helped to make possible.

It was not however until after 1060 that William's position in Gaul began rapidly to be transformed and in such a manner as might vitally affect his relations with England. In that year the deaths of King Henry I and Count Geoffrey of Anjou freed him from his two most formidable opponents in France, while Philip I the new king of France who was a boy, was placed under the tutelage of the duke's Flemish father-in-law. In 1063, the death of Count Walter of Maine, who was the Confessor's nephew, removed a possible claimant to the English succession, and the acquisition of Maine itself by the duke of Normandy further altered the balance of political power in northern France to his advantage. The famous visit which Harold earl of Wessex made to Normandy, as it seems in 1064, whatever may have been its motives, was to prove of even greater importance, since the resulting oath sworn by Harold to

William was understood throughout western Europe as pledging the earl to support the claim of the duke to England, or at all events not to oppose it. Again, the successful Norman expedition against Brittany in the same year minimized the threat of resistance in the west, while the Northumbrian revolt of 1065 indicated what was to be the chief weakness of his principal adversary in England. When, therefore, on 5 January 1066 there occurred the death of the childless king of England, and on the very next day Earl Harold seized the English throne, William's policy towards England was brought to its test at a time peculiarly favourable to its fulfilment.

Political power, thus consistently developed controlled and extended by a great duke, made it possible for the conquest of an ancient kingdom to be attempted. But it does not of itself suffice to explain *why* the venture was undertaken; nor does it account for its peculiar consequences. The crisis of 1066 is not to be viewed simply as a struggle between three princes contending for a throne; and though a lust for plunder (which was later to be abundantly sated) undoubtedly fired the Norman followers of William, this does not by itself account for the consequences to England of the Norman conquest. Again, if the Norman success in arms derived in large measure from the recent increase of Norman power under Duke William, this alone cannot explain the support which the duke received from outside Normandy, or for the ultimate results of the policy which he was to bring to fruition in England.

The character of the propaganda which William employed in 1066, and which was so materially to assist him thus also deserves examination in this respect. This propaganda, it will be recalled, was informed throughout by moral and ecclesiastical sentiments. The murder of Alfred Atheling in 1036 called (it was said) for divine vengeance on the son of his murderer. Stigand, a schismatic archbishop, occupied the throne of St Augustine. The solemn promise of a venerated king had been abrogated, and a solemn oath sworn upon relics demanded the punishment of Heaven on the perjured usurper. We are not here concerned, of course, with the falsity or truth of these assertions. What is notable is firstly the character of William's propaganda at this juncture, and secondly the extent to which it was accepted in western Europe. As is well known, the Norman case was successfully stated at Rome, and in the event William was to fight at Hastings under a papal banner and with consecrated relics round his neck.

The Norman expedition had in fact been made to appear in the nature of a holy war, and so it was to be widely regarded. This is usually considered as a triumph for William's diplomacy, and this in truth it was. But it was a claim that was particularly attuned to contemporary Norman sentiments, and was indeed probably inspired by them. For the latter half of the eleventh century was emphatically the time when the notion of a holy war was continuously and widely exploited in Norman interests. Again and again the same theme was stressed. In 1059 the Normans Robert Guiscard and Richard of Capua, becoming vassals of the Holy See, had pledged themselves to its defence. In 1062 Pope Alexander II had given his blessing and a banner to Norman knights fighting in Sicily. In 1064 according to both French and Arab sources, the Normans were especially prominent in the 'crusade of Barbastro' in Spain. In 1066 the same Alexander II gave William his blessing and a banner for the expedition to England. Between 1060 and 1070 the Normans (though with very diverse motives) were achieving in Sicily what was in fact to prove the most important victory of Christians over Moslems in the eleventh century. In 1070 William was to be solemnly proclaimed by papal legates at Winchester, and in 1072 while William was advancing into

Scotland, Roger son of Tancred captured Palermo from the Saracens.

These events were, moreover, closely connected, not only in time but also in spirit, for (as must be emphasized) they were conducted by men who were brothers and cousins of each other, and fully conscious of their relationship and their common purpose. William the Conqueror is said to have been wont to refresh his courage by contemplating the achievements of Robert Guiscard, and the name of Grandmesnil was as famous in Apulia as it was to become at Leicester. John, abbot of Fécamp, mediated between Pope Leo IX and Richard of Capua, while Geoffrey, bishop of Coutances, received from his relatives in Italy contributions towards the building of his cathedral at home. The Norman warriors of this age were avid of plunder and stained with brigandage, but they were none the less conscious of belonging to an integrated Norman world which was proud of its armed might, and also of its self-asserted Christian mission. Its exploits had before 1066 already stretched from Spain through Apulia to Constantinople, from Brittany to the Taurus, and they were soon to extend from Abernethy to Syracuse. Here was a vast zone of interconnected endeavour comparable even to that of the fabled Charlemagne in the *Song of Roland*. The sentiments it inspired coloured all Norman policy at this time. And, in a real sense, this far-flung extension of Norman power reached its climax in Sussex in October 1066.

William's expedition to England in the autumn of 1066, the campaign which followed and the battle which was its culmination are to be described elsewhere in this book, as will also be the social and political consequences to England of the Norman conquest. The purpose of the foregoing remarks has been simply to indicate the extent to which William's success in 1066 may be related to what he had earlier achieved in the development of Norman power and policy. And it will now be further suggested that the political developments which took place between 1066 and 1087 under his rule as king may likewise be related to what he had previously achieved as duke. The interconnected movements which under William, as duke, had created the strength of Normandy in 1066 we have discovered to be aristocratic, ecclesiastical and ducal. The chief directions in which Norman influence was exercised in England during the reign of William as king may fairly be described as aristocratic, ecclesiastical and royal.

The most striking social consequence of the Norman conquest was undoubtedly the aristocratic revolution which involved the tragic downfall of the Old-English nobility and its replacement by a new secular aristocracy imported from overseas. The magnitude of the change and the vast spoliation it involved are well documented, and they can be considered quite apart from the vexed question of the origins of feudal organization in England. Those members of the Old-English nobility which in 1066 escaped the slaughters of Fulford, Stamford Bridge and Hastings faced a bleak future as the defeated supporters of a lost cause, and they suffered further misfortunes in the early wars of William's English reign which ended any policy of compromise which the new king might have been disposed to adopt towards them. The result was catastrophic. The collapse of the Old-English nobility was almost complete by the end of William's reign. It has been estimated that in 1086 only about 8 per cent of the land of England remained in the possession of this class. It had ceased to be an integral part of English society.

The substitution in its place of an aristocracy which was overwhelmingly Norman in origin has likewise been fully established. But the statement needs some qualification in that, even as the expedition had been widely supported in Europe, so also did many of the new holders of English lands come from outside Normandy. Flemings for instance were prominent among them, particularly perhaps in the north, and it was a man from Flanders, Gerbod, who, about 1070 became the first Earl of Chester. More important still were the Bretons who had followed the Conqueror to England. The great honour of Richmond (Yorkshire) with its 400 dependent manors was given to a member of the comital house of Brittany, and it was a Breton, Ralph of Gael who, perhaps as early as 1067 was made earl of Norfolk. The significance of the non-Norman element in the aristocracy set up by William in England should therefore not be minimized, but this was none the less always subordinate, and political events were soon to diminish its importance. The hostility of Flanders to the Anglo-Norman kingdom which grew after 1067 immediately detracted from the Flemish influence on England, and Gerbod, earl of Chester, having fought in the battle of Cassel, disappeared from the English scene, and was replaced as earl by Hugh son of Richard, *vicomte* of Avranches. In like manner, the suppression of the rebellion of the earls in 1075 was said to have 'purged' England from Breton influence, and while Ralph of Gael thereafter ceased to be earl of Norfolk, so also did Brian of Brittany then make way in Cornwall for the Conqueror's half-brother Robert, count of Mortain.

The aristocracy imposed upon England by William the Conqueror was in fact to be overwhelmingly representative of just that aristocracy which had arisen in Normandy between 1040 and 1066. By 1086 nearly half the land of England had passed into the possession of this class, and about half of this (namely a quarter of the total) had been given to only eleven men, of whom all but two were Normans who had been identified with the young duke during his early career. And the same is true of the more important personages by whom they were surrounded: the representatives of the comital houses of Eu and Evreux; Roger Bigot from Calvados; Robert Malet from the neighbourhood of Evreux; Robert and Henry the sons of Roger of Beaumont on the Risle. It is an impressive list, but while of course it could be supplemented, it could not be very widely extended. The important secular tenants of English lands in 1086 probably numbered less than two hundred. And from among these the greater men and the greater families stand out to testify to the manner in which the territorial wealth of England had been acquired by the leading members of that aristocracy which had obtained power in Normandy under Duke William.

The cohesion which had earlier been achieved by this group in Normandy, and its association with William, were likewise to be reproduced in England. Indeed the Conqueror's success in retaining his conjoint realm between 1066 and 1087 was due in no small measure to the maintenance of that unity of purpose between William and his magnates which had been attained in Normandy before the Conquest. After 1066 as before, it remained as much to the interest of these men as to the Conqueror himself that dissensions among them should not be allowed to develop. The rebellion of 1075 received no general support from the Norman nobility, and in 1079 elder members of the same aristocracy took common action to recall to their allegiance cadet members of their own families who had supported the revolt of the king's son Robert against his father. It was a violent age dominated by the rivalries of highly competitive families. But a recognition of mutual obligations by the king and his magnates both in England and in Normandy assisted the Anglo-Norman kingdom to survive, and went far to determine its character.

In ecclesiastical affairs also a similar relationship can be discerned between William's reign in England and his previous rule of Normandy. The church in England between 1070 and 1087 under the control of William was to experience great changes, many of which tended to make it conform more closely to the pattern which had previously taken shape in the Province of Rouen. Whether these changes were good or bad is not of course here in question: nor need it be debated whether the loss of a fine vernacular culture which was involved was compensated by a closer relation between England and those intellectual movements in western Europe which were contributing to the renaissance of the twelfth century. The connexion between the ecclesiastical development of Normandy and England during the Conqueror's lifetime is however apparent. Between 1066 and 1087 the reformed monasteries of Normandy gave no less than twenty-two abbots and five bishops to England; and even as William as duke had controlled the Norman church so also did he now, in co-operation with his great Archbishop Lanfranc, make himself responsible for the changes in England. All major appointments (most of which were good) were in practice in his hands, and the bishoprics of England were very generally in his time to assume the form they were to retain until the Reformation. Most notable of all was the royal participation in the work of ecclesiastical councils which now began to be a regular feature of church life in the kingdom as in the duchy. Thus, William took part in the councils at Winchester in 1070, 1072 and 1076; at Rouen in 1074; at Lillebonne in 1080, and at Gloucester in 1085. This was evidently a ruler who in the words of Professor Knowles 'was resolved of set purpose to raise the whole level of ecclesiastical discipline in his dominions'.[1]

It was in fact the domination he sought to exercise over the church which in part explains his ambivalent attitude towards

[1] David Knowles, *Monastic Order in England* (1940), p. 93.

the papacy. He had come to England with papal support; he could claim with some justice to be the sponsor of those reforms which with papal approval were beginning to pervade the western church. But as in Normandy so also now in England he would not abandon the rights over the church which he held to be inherent in his office. The opposition was clear cut and fundamental; it was to be productive of long-enduring controversies. But its implications during William's lifetime should not be overstressed. In one respect William's disputes with Gregory VII were concerned with the means by which might be implemented a policy of ecclesiastical reform which they shared in common. There was more co-operation than controversy between William and the papacy. Relations might be strained almost to breaking point, but the pope with whom William contended could none the less praise his zeal for religion.

In conformity with the earlier growth of Normandy under Duke William the Norman impact upon England after 1066 was thus in the first instance to be aristocratic and ecclesiastical. It was, however, to be more specifically royal, in the sense that it was dependent upon the work of a duke who had become a king. The coronation of William at Westminster on Christmas Day 1066 was not only the central event of his life: it foreshadowed the character of his rule in England. By becoming a king, William assumed all the semi-sacred prestige which the men of the time were disposed to give to the royal office, and this had deep Norman implications since it could be easily related to the religious sanctions which had been so widely claimed for Norman enterprise. At the same time a wider gulf was placed between him and even the greatest of his followers, and he was thereby to be assisted in his endeavour to hold together as a single political entity his dominions on both sides of the Channel. As a sanctified king he could moreover exercise

F

over the church a closer control with a greater appearance of legitimacy. And his position among the other secular rulers of western Europe was transformed.

This was, however, only part of the matter. William in 1066 became not only a king: he became more specifically king of the English (*Rex Anglorum*). He was hallowed by a rite substantially identical with that which had been employed in the coronation of English kings from at least the time of Edgar. As a result his Norman policy which we have watched was now brought into contact with a distinct complex of loyalties, some religious, some traditional, but all emotionally compelling. The policy itself thus at once began to be modified, and in the more practical sphere William was enabled to assume all the powers, and much of the prestige, which had formerly been vested in Old-English royalty. It was a mark of his astute appraisal of the situation that, from the start of his rule in England, he claimed to be the legitimate successor of Edward the Confessor. The reign of Harold II was treated as a usurpation – as an inter-regnum.

Such claims, exercised and developed at the hands of a man who was also a great constructive statesman, were in fact to entail remarkable and unexpected results. William was a con-queror; his advent into England was a cause of spoilation; in the English church and in the higher ranks of secular society it entailed revolutionary change. But, in many respects, William could also be considered as a conservative, and it was a mark of his political genius that he could adapt to his purpose the in-stitutions of the land he had won by invasion. As *Rex Anglorum* he used the royal system of administration. His writs are substantially identical in form with those of Edward the Confessor, though they came soon to be couched in Latin rather than in the vernacular. He employed the sheriff as his chief executive officer in local government though the shrievalty became progressively Norman in composition. He gave fresh vitality to the courts of shire and hundred, and he utilized (with ruthless efficiency) the taxational system that he found in this country. Most of his earliest charters were concerned to insist that the customs which had prevailed in the Confessor's time should be respected, and this injunction was consistently to be repeated and very often enforced. In the great trials, which were so marked a feature of his reign, appeal was constantly made to Old-English law, and it was partly for this reason that the great transference of landed property which the Conquest entailed was carried out without general anarchy. Even in the church, where the changes were very far-reaching, respect was paid to Old-English traditions, particularly with regard to the rights of the See of Canterbury. It was, in short, directly due to William himself – the duke who had become a king – and a king of the English – that the Norman conquest proved almost as important for what it preserved as for what it created.

It is assuredly no part of the purpose of this short essay to describe the constitutional and administrative history of England during the reign of William the Conqueror. But any estimate of William's character and career must take note of the fact that what he wrought in England was accomplished in the midst of incessant warfare. The formation of the Anglo-Norman kingdom which was the immediate result of William's victory altered the balance of political power in western Europe in such a manner as to provoke a continuous and relentless opposition that was bent on its destruction. Paris and Anjou, Scandinavia and Scotland were immediately and directly effected, and William's conjoint realm was in fact only to survive by means of an unremitting military effort which extended over two decades.

Looking back on that prolonged defence, which was so strongly to affect the English future, its chief feature may well seem to have been the inherent inter-dependence of all its parts. The suppression of risings in England was always connected with the persisting threat of attack from Scandinavia or Scotland from Anjou or Maine, and the protection of the northern frontier beyond Yorkshire could never be dissociated from the active hostility which was manifested in France or Flanders or beyond the North Sea. It was, moreover, characteristic of this situation that after 1070 the attack directed against the Anglo-Norman realm should have been ever more closely co-ordinated by the astute diplomacy of Philip I of France whose object throughout was to disrupt the political union of Normandy and England – which was in fact to be achieved for seventeen years after William's death. The preservation of his rule in England, and the maintenance of the unity of the Anglo-Norman kingdom, must always have seemed to William to involve a single problem; and the related campaigns of the king and his lieutenants had a common purpose, whether they were waged in Northumbria or Maine, or whether they were directed against Sweyn Estrithson of Denmark or Fulk le Rechin of Anjou, King Malcolm of Scotland or King Philip of France.

The point perhaps deserves more emphasis than it always receives, and it could be plentifully illustrated. The claims of Edgar Atheling to the English throne were for instance to be sponsored successively by King Malcolm and King Philip. The rising of the north in 1069–70 was supported by a fleet from Scandinavia which was to operate off the coast of England for four years. The revolt of Maine began almost simultaneously with the Yorkshire rebellion, and culminated in 1072 with the establishment of Fulk le Rechin at Le Mans. Again, in 1075, the rebellion of the earls in England was led by a Breton earl of Norfolk, and though it was suppressed in England, the war that it initiated was continued in Brittany, and ended with William's defeat at Dol – a reverse which was to rob him of the initiative in France for a decade. Once again, the news of William's repulse before the walls of Gerberoi in 1079 by King Philip and William's son, Robert, had no sooner spread to Scotland than King Malcolm of Scotland raided Northumbria and started the rising which led to the murder of Bishop Walchere and the temporary collapse of Norman authority in the north.

The same pattern of politics was in fact to persist until the end of the reign. It was entirely characteristic of the earlier defence of the Anglo-Norman realm that during the last twenty months of his life, William should have faced not only the threat of a combined attack from Scandinavia and Flanders – from Cnut IV of Denmark and Count Robert of Flanders – but that he should also have been constrained to conduct his final campaign on the south-eastern frontier of Normandy against the king of France. During these months, and in connexion with this crisis, he initiated the Domesday Survey, and convoked the Salisbury Moot. But he met his lethal injury at Mantes in the Vexin, and early in the morning of 9 September 1087 he died within sound of the church bells of Rouen.

At the close of this astonishing career it is tempting to contemplate the character of the extraordinary man who made it. To do so is not, however, easy, since such diverse judgements have been passed upon William, and he had no intimate biographer who could examine his motives, or probe his private thoughts. He must be judged by his acts, but his acts are sufficiently illuminating. They leave no doubt of his greatness, but they reveal also a man who was harsh and unlovable – perhaps even personally repellent. Most of his life was spent in war, and war brought out what was brutal in this burly warrior whose physical strength (until diminished by corpulence) was exceptional, and who may have looked something like Henry VIII of England. His savagery in war is well attested. The horrors of Alençon in 1052 were matched by those which he inflicted on Mantes in 1087, and his devastation of the Home Counties in 1066 was a fit prelude to his harrying of the north in 1070. Yet it may be questioned whether William, as a warrior, was more brutal than most of his contemporaries, or that he had a blunter sense of ethics or humanity than many of his successors in war down to the twentieth century. And if many of his acts in this respect cannot be excused, they can at least be explained. The sack of Alençon made certain the bloodless surrender of Domfront; the isolation of London in 1066 was based upon considered strategy; and there were many occasions when William went out of his way (as in Normandy in 1066, and at Exeter in 1068) to prevent plundering by his troops. The horrible devastation of northern England in 1070 is in truth impossible to palliate, but it took place at a crisis when the Anglo-Norman kingdom was threatened from Northumbria and Scotland from Norway and from Maine. As to the New Forest it might perhaps be remarked that William was not the first – nor the last – king in England to lay waste a countryside for his sport.

As a warrior, William was (perhaps inevitably) stained with blood. As a ruler, his avarice was notorious, and his taxation savage. He needed money for his government, and particularly for the numerous mercenaries he employed. The ruthlessness with which he extracted money from England must be set against the good administration he provided. Here, too, however, a balanced judgement is necessary. If William was 'stern beyond measure', there were many who benefited thereby. It was not for nothing that a panic spread among lesser folk when they heard of his death, for they were aware of the disorders which were likely to follow his passing, and it was an Englishman who knew him, who, at the last, after lamenting his harshness, paid tribute to the good order he maintained. Ruthless in war, he was not a bloodthirsty brute. Strong in rule, he was not a tyrant. Contemporaries found him a man to fear, but also a man to respect.

The basis of his achievement was his genius for leadership. Reference is often made to the good fortune which he some-times enjoyed, as in the deaths of his two chief rivals in France in 1060, and in certain of the circumstances of 1066. But no reference to luck can possibly be adequate to explain a career of this character, or an achievement of this magnitude. There must have been a wonderful strength of personality in this man who could rise from his bastard beginnings to such power, and who could elicit from the hard-faced men who surrounded him, both in Normandy and England, such a constant measure of support. He was harsh and rapacious, personally pious, courageous in adversity, and indomitably tenacious of purpose. He could suit his policy to opportunity; but his will was inflexible, and his energy was untiring. Thus between 1051 and 1054, when in his middle twenties, he captured Alençon and Domfront, reduced the stronghold of Arques, repelled a great invasion by the French king, held an important ecclesiastical council and deposed an Archbishop of Rouen. Again, at a later stage of his career, only a matter of months elapsed between his invasion of Scotland late in 1072 and his campaign in Maine in the next year. He was ever on the move, and if both his vices and his virtues were exceptional, so also were the con-ditions in which his life was spent. His vigorous leadership pervaded his whole career, and not least the last two years of his life when so much was accomplished. This quality alone made possible not only his survival as duke, but also the existence and preservation of the Anglo-Norman kingdom, which he established. As Professor Southern has justly remarked, 'he had an unrivalled mastery of the problems of the secular world – that is to say of other men's wills – in both fighting and ruling unapproached in creative power by any other medieval ruler after Charlemagne'.[1]

It would, in truth, be difficult to deny to William the Conqueror a place among the greatest monarchs of the Middle Ages. He stands four-square, a dominant figure against the background of his own fascinating and tumultuous age. As a warrior he was widely renowned, and probably justly, for if his later campaigns in France were undistinguished, his earlier siege operations in Maine were notable, and in the great enterprise of 1066 his patience, his organization and his generalship were surely of the highest order. But it is above all for his constructive statesmanship that he commands attention; and here his achievement must appear all the more remarkable when it is recalled that his ceaseless preoccupation with the problems of government was coupled with ceaseless campaigning. The results of his rule had enduring consequences which stretched even beyond the confines of his own wide dominions. He adapted his policy to a crisis which, in his time, affected Scandinavia and Italy, France and England; and the development of western Europe in the Middle Ages was substantially affected by what he accomplished. In Normandy he brought a distracted province to a new peak of strength. To England he gave a new aristocracy and a reconstituted church. At the same time, he was concerned to respect the traditions of the country he conquered, and he revitalized many of its ancient institutions. He made his own contribution to the highly individual character of medieval England, and Anglo-Norman history in the eleventh century cannot be appraised without reference to his characteristic acts.

[1] R. W. Southern, *Saint Anselm and his Biographer* (1963), p. 4.

III · The Campaign of 1066

by Lieutenant-Colonel CHARLES H. LEMMON, DSO

late Royal Artillery
President, The Battle and District Historical Society

After the coronation of King Harold, and the appearance of Halley's Comet, the next episode depicted on the Bayeux Tapestry is the arrival of a ship in Normandy. The date must have been about 10 January 1066. The ship carries a crew of three and an individual who seems to be in a hurry to disembark. He was a messenger, doubtless one of the many Normans living in England; and he brought the astounding news that Edward the Confessor had died on 5 January and that Harold Godwinson had been crowned king of England the very next day. The messenger found Duke William hunting in the park of Quévilly near Rouen, and in the very act, so it is said, of drawing his bow. William returned at once to his hall, where he is reported to have given the matter long and anxious thought, which resulted in his sending an embassy to Harold on 15 January. From the various conflicting accounts nothing definite can be stated about the terms either of William's message or of Harold's answer; but it may be surmised that the former was a challenge of Harold's right to the crown, and the latter its summary rejection. The mission was fruitless, Harold's accession was a *fait accompli* and the matter had passed beyond negotiation. From that moment William must have realized that nothing short of a successful full-scale invasion of England could ever place the crown of that country on his head. A full-scale invasion of England, however, would be far

Normandy in the Eleventh Century

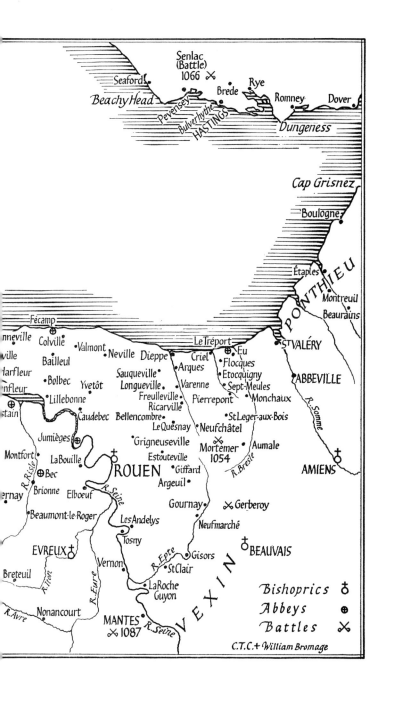

Senlac
(Battle)
1066 ⚔
Seaford
Beachy Head
Pevensey Bulverhythe
HASTINGS
Brede Rye
Romney Dover
Dungeness

Cap Grisnez

Boulogne

Étaples
Montreuil
Beaurains
Fécamp
PONTHIEU
ST VALÉRY
ABBEVILLE

nneville Colville
ville Bailleul
Harfleur ●Bolbec Yvetôt
nfleur ●Lillebonne
stain ●Caudebec
Jumièges
Montfort● LaBouille
Brionne Elbeuf
rnay ●Beaumont-le-Roger
●Valmont Neville Dieppe
Sauqueville
Longueville
Freulleville
Ricarville
Bellencombre●
LeQuesnay
Grigneuseville
Estouteville
ROUEN †
●Giffard
Argueil●
Criel
Arques
●Flocques
●Etocquigny
●Sept-Meules
Pierrepont ●Monchaux
●St Leger-aux-Bois
●Neufchâtel
Mortemer● Aumale
1054
R.Bresle
R.Somme
AMIENS †

Eu
Varenne

Gournay● ⚔ Gerberoy
Les Andelys
Tosny
EVREUX †
Breteuil
Nonancourt
Vernon
LaRoche
Guyon
MANTES
⚔1087
R.Seine
R.Epte
●Gisors
●StClair
Neufmarché
VEXIN
† BEAUVAIS

Bishoprics †
Abbeys ⊕
Battles ⚔

C.T.C.✝ William Bromage

beyond anything which he had hitherto attempted. Normans, it is true, had carried out overseas expeditions before, notably to Sicily. With great coolness they had embarked on the conquest of countries where they were far outnumbered by the native population; but this expedition would necessarily have to be on a larger scale, and the potential odds against its success would be greater. The English possessed fighting forces which were by no means negligible: a few thousand highly-trained professional Housecarls, probably the finest soldiers in Europe, backed by a Fyrd, or national militia, the potential strength of which, since every five hides of land had to produce one man, might be as high as 48,000. That the landing would be opposed was only to be expected. Julius Caesar, with two legions comprising about 10,000 highly-trained professional soldiers, carried in ninety-eight transports and escorted by armed triremes, had only landed with difficulty, could not establish himself in the island and was lucky to be able to re-embark. With an inadequate number of purely Norman troops, and without means of transporting an army across the Channel, the difficulties of invading England might well seem insuperable to many on whose support of the project William would be compelled to rely. Setting aside the difficulties, the project, from a strategic point of view, exceeded any prudent degree of 'calculated risk'.

William could not hope to raise sufficient men and ships without outside help; but first he had to deal with his own barons, who might consider themselves not bound by their feudal tenure to follow him overseas for the purpose of making him king of England. His first step was therefore to lay the matter before fourteen of his relations and most trusted councillors. This inner council approved the purpose of the expedition and pledged their support; but considered that the concurrence of all the barons of Normandy was necessary. Such a meeting was convened at Lillebonne. After reciting his rights, and the wrongs which Harold had done, William attempted to bounce the assembly by saying that he would not ask whether they would help him in such a cause. He took their zeal and loyalty for granted; and he asked only how many ships and men each would bring as a freewill offering. The barons did not see matters in that light at all, raised all sorts of objections, and eventually the meeting broke up in disorder.

Thereafter there followed a demonstration of that indefinable power which has been given from time to time to military commanders who have differed widely in personality: the power to draw men to them who will accept their leadership with complete confidence, and follow them wherever they may lead. William interviewed each baron separately: an arduous task, as the number must have exceeded one hundred. One by one they yielded to his persuasions, and agreed not only to serve him in his enterprise, but on this occasion, for once, to double their normal feudal obligations. Immediately each baron had given his promise a clerk entered in a book the number of ships and men that he would supply. The net was then spread more widely; and William invited soldiers from every quarter to come as volunteers, offering them the spoils of the campaign as an inducement. His negotiations with rulers of states are somewhat obscure: apparently he met King Philip of France personally, sent embassies to the Emperor Henry III and the king of Denmark, and approached his father-in-law, Baldwin of Flanders. Neither Philip nor Baldwin would, as rulers, give any help; but the fact remains that a large number of volunteers came from both their states; and these, with those collected by Eustace, count of Boulogne, brother-in-law of Edward the Confessor, were formed into a division under the command of the Norman, Roger of Montgomerie. The most that William seems to have obtained from the emperor was a promise not to hinder recruitment of volunteers in the Empire, and from the king of Denmark his neutrality. The latter was apparently not kept, as Danish volunteers are said to have formed part of Harold's army. From Brittany, the neighbouring and nominally vassal state, came the largest contingent of troops which was not Norman; and these were organized as a division under the command of Alan Fergant, cousin of Conan, the reigning count. It has been suggested that the eagerness of the Celtic Bretons to invade Britain was due to a desire to avenge their ancestors whom the Saxons had driven from the island.

With Pope Alexander II William obtained signal success. His cause was pleaded by the archdeacon of Lisieux on the grounds of Harold's alleged perjury. A conclave was held, at which Harold was declared a usurper, and William the lawful successor of Edward the Confessor. The pope bestowed his blessing on the expedition, sending William a consecrated banner. In effect, he made the expedition a crusade; which greatly aided the recruitment of the expeditionary force.

Individual recruits now came in from many lands – mostly soldiers of fortune and mere adventurers attracted by the hope of plunder. It would be from these that the mercenary men-at-arms and archers were enrolled. Norman armies in the past had consisted almost entirely of cavalry; but this time, it is clear from passages in the chronicles, owing to the difficulty of transporting horses, a large proportion had of necessity to be archers and heavy infantry; a form of service which was beneath the dignity of knights and their followers.

The Bayeux Tapestry passes over the raising of the army, and the next scene is headed *Here Duke William ordered ships to be built*. We are shown how his orders were carried out, the trees being felled, the planks being cut and stacked, the shipwrights at work and the finished ships being launched by block and tackle. Shipbuilding occupied the summer of 1066 until about 12 August, when those completed were assembled at the port of Dives. The number promised had been 752; but Wace states that his father told him there were only 696. Wace, the poet who wrote the *Roman de Rou* a century after the event, is not a reliable military historian; but his figure, the lowest of any chronicler, is credible, and General James used it as a basis to estimate the strength of the forces which crossed the Channel. Other sources James used were *Eccleston's Antiquities*, which gives details of the English overseas expeditions of the thirteenth and fourteenth centuries when the largest ships carried only forty-four men, the chroniclers' lists of ship-donors and the Bayeux Tapestry, on which only five of the twelve ships shown carry horses. His findings, published in the *Royal Engineers' Journal* for January 1907, were that 400 of the ships each carried nine men with horses, and that the remaining 296 ships each carried an average of twenty-five dismounted men, making his total estimate 11,000 men, which would include sailors, sutlers and camp followers, as the number carried across the channel. Sir James Ramsay's esti-mate in 1898 had been 10,000; and William's boast to Robert the son of Wymarc may not be without significance: 'If I had only 10,000 men, such as the 60,000 I have, I would still go on.'

The ships specially built for the expedition must be regarded rather as 'landing craft' than troop transports. They could have been hardly the size of coastal fishing boats, and more akin to the 'Prames' on which Bonaparte hoped to carry his invading troops across the channel, though even these carried eighty men each. They were much smaller than Julius Caesar's *nave onerariae* which carried 120 legionaries. A curiosity of the ship-building programme is that no 'warships' or armed vessels to serve as escort are mentioned. Caesar protected his transports with armed triremes; while Bonaparte cancelled all his invasion

G

plans because he could not achieve command of the sea. Harold's fleet was in the channel during the Norman ship-building; though it was, as it happened, withdrawn before the invasion. William attempted no blockade and took a big risk in ignoring command of the sea.

Ships such as those shown on the Bayeux Tapestry must have needed the wind very nearly astern; so that to sail across the channel from Dives a due south wind, which is rather unusual, was necessary. The wind blew obstinately from the west for a whole month; at the end of which time, about 12 September, William decided to use it to sail up the coast to St Valery at the mouth of the Somme, whence the fleet would have a shorter passage, and be able to cross with a south-east wind. The voyage along the 100 miles of coast must have been hazardous; for William of Poitiers records 'terrible ship-wrecks'. One would hardly suppose that the whole army was embarked for this move: the cavalry at least would have marched.

In England, the Fyrd, or militia, had been keeping watch on the south coast all through the summer. The number assigned to this task is unlikely to have been more than one quarter of the potential strength of the Fyrd in the whole country, or say 12,000. Of these, each individual could be called up, when there was no fighting to be done, for two months only. On 8 September the supply of fyrdmen must have run out; for on that date, only a few days before the Norman fleet moved to St Valery, the last elements of the Fyrd were disembodied. The theory that the fyrdmen were required to help with the harvest is hardly tenable; because on 14 September, which is the New Style equivalent of their disembodiment date, the harvest in a normal year is nearly or quite completed.

At the same time, the fleet was sent to London and paid off; and nothing definite can be gleaned from the chronicles that it ever met the Norman fleet in combat, or interfered with the invasion.

Then a heavy blow fell. On or about 15 September, Harald Hardrada, king of Norway, landed at Riccal on the bank of the Yorkshire Ouse. His shadowy claim to the English throne was based on an alleged agreement in 1038 between his predecessor Magnus and Harthacnut, king of Denmark, before the latter had become king of England. On 20 September he heavily defeated the northern earls Edwin and Morcar at the battle of Fulford. Intelligence was good in medieval warfare; and Harold may quite possibly have heard, in London, at some time from 18 September to the 20th, both of the Norwegian landing and of the increased threat arising from the Norman change of embarkation port. He must have issued immediate orders for the re-embodiment of the Fyrd, and left London with his Housecarls not later than the 20th, since he arrived at Tadcaster on 24 September. News of the defeat of Edwin and Morcar must have reached him while on the march; but although his Housecarls, numbering at most 3,000, could have received but little reinforcement from the Fyrd, owing to shortness of time, he pushed on at the high march-rate of nearly forty miles a day along the Roman road to York expecting to find the Norwegians there. Actually, for no very apparent reason, they had moved out to Stamford Bridge eight miles further on; where Harold fell upon them on 25 September and destroyed almost their entire army. Harald Hardrada and his own renegade brother Tostig were killed; and the victorious army, which itself had suffered heavy casualties, then returned to York to rest and celebrate.

The weather on the other side of the Channel was cold and wet, and the wind remained in the west until 27 September, when it suddenly changed to the east. The ships were loaded and the troops embarked with all speed. The Bayeux Tapestry shows helmets, hauberks, axes, swords and lances being carried down to the ships; while provisions are also indicated by men carrying a ham and a barrel. A curious hand-wagon, which we are told carried both wine and arms, is an example, perhaps, of the combined Ordnance and Supply vehicles which accompanied the forces.

The sun set at 5.34 pm that day, and the crescent moon (six days old) also set at about 9.15 pm, so that it was necessary to be out on the open sea by 6.30 pm. William ordered a masthead light to be hoisted on every ship, that the ships should keep together and that all should heave-to for a while in the middle of the night. The reason for the latter was that the period of darkness was too long for both the embarkation and the landing to be made in daylight. The order to set sail again after the heave-to was given by hoisting a masthead light on *Mora*, the duke's flagship, and by the sounding of trumpets. How the fleet was ordered to heave-to we are not told, nor how the ships managed to keep together on a moonless night without frequent collisions and consequent damage. Wind and sea conditions appear to have been ideal; it began to get light again about 5 am and the sun rose at 6.4 am. William's flagship, which had been given him by his wife Matilda, had outdistanced the rest of the fleet and had to heave-to again; some anxiety being caused until a lookout at the masthead reported ships in view. The voyage continued, and the English coast was reached at Pevensey Level about 8.30 am. So ended this very remarkable voyage which for its boldness of conception, the magnitude of the task involved and the efficiency with which it was carried out with the primitive shipping of the eleventh century, does not seem to have received the recognition as an operation of war which it undoubtedly deserves. Only two vessels were lost; one of which, at least, must have come ashore, as recorded, at Romney in Kent, where the inhabitants killed all the occupants. In one of the ships there perished the official southsayer of the expedition who, the duke declared, was not much loss, as he had been unable to predict his own fate.

While the chroniclers leave little doubt that the Norman fleet reached the coast near Pevensey, their accounts of the landing and subsequent movements of troops are obscure and conflicting; so that it is necessary to consider how the land probably lay in 1066 before a reconstruction can be made.

Pevensey Level,[1] formed by the combined effect of the great thaw after the last Ice Age, and the west to east sea drift, is now a roughly semi-circular plain about six miles in diameter, mostly of grazing land intersected by drainage channels and separated from the sea by a high bank of shingle. Although in the thirteenth century the sea flowed freely over it, there were, two centuries earlier, as Domesday Book shows, large culti-vated areas, like those still to be seen on the Essex coast, which became islands in an expanse of shallow water at high tide; and were separated at low tide by mud flats and winding water channels, across which causeways had probably been built. Into this area a peninsula projects from the western side. It is three miles long, and behind it in 1066, as in Roman times, lay a sheltered harbour. On the point of this peninsula the Romans had built the fortress of Anderida, whose walls still stand to a height of 25 feet, and the Saxons the seaport and market town of Pevensey, which was small but important enough to levy harbour dues. A Roman road westward to Lewes and London provided the sole communication inland.

In 1066 a ship entering Pevensey harbour would first pass through a wide gap in the shingle bank, then follow the chan-nel through the tidal mud-flats, round the peninsula, and cast anchor in the harbour close under the north walls of Anderida

[1] I am indebted to Miss M. A. Ash for this information.

(now Pevensey Castle). The chroniclers are generally agreed that the duke himself landed at Pevensey 'at the third hour' which, as time is now reckoned, works out at 8.57 am. One account, however, states that disembarkation took place at intervals along the shore; and another that the invaders seized the shore of the sea, thus indicating landings on the shingle bank, where it would have been easy to run ships ashore to land infantry, but difficult to disembark the horses. Unfortunately the portion of the tapestry which shows the landing of horses gives no clue to the method employed. (See illustration, plate 5a.) We may suppose that the ships carrying the duke, with such cavalry as accompanied him, as well as the troops detailed to garrison Pevensey, entered the harbour, where there may have been wharves; and that the remainder were run ashore at various points along the shingle bank and beach towards Hastings. Again there is general agreement among the chroniclers that the duke moved his army to Hastings with very little delay. As the shingle bank would provide the inhabitants with a means of crossing the marsh, one presumes that there was some track behind it whereby troops landing on it eastward of the harbour mouth could reach solid ground about Coding, which is now called Cooden, and then march to Hastings. Those, however, who landed on the western side of the harbour, or at Pevensey itself, would have to cross to the eastern side. The usually accepted theory is that they marched around the whole perimeter of Pevensey Level, a distance of twenty-six miles. While several villages near the northern edge of the Level were undoubtedly devastated, this could have been done by raiding parties, and does not prove that any large part of the army passed that way; nor would the duke have been likely to divide his forces in that manner. William of Poitiers records an incident which may have a bearing on the question. Immediately after landing, William carried out a reconnaissance accompanied by not more than twenty-five men. The by-paths were so rough that they had to dismount, and William himself carried the corslets of two of his companions, presumably because they were exhausted. Since the Roman road to Lewes, the sole link with the mainland, could hardly have been in the condition described, the incident suggests two things: firstly, that William did not plan to march inland by the Lewes road; and secondly, that he searched without success among the rough tracks leading to islands in the marsh for a way round the end of the harbour by which to unite his army and march to Hastings. There is a possible alternative to a march around the perimeter of the marsh, which is that after the garrison of Pevensey had been installed, the rest of the troops who had landed there, not many in number, re-embarked, dropped down the river with the tide and proceeded to Hastings by rowing if the wind did not serve. The bulk of the cavalry could either have been ordered beforehand to make the port of Hastings if possible; or the horses could have been left aboard their transports in harbour until the result of the reconnaissance was known.

Although the Saxon army was unable to offer any opposition to the Norman landing, on account of the withdrawal of the Fyrd, an excellently organized lookout system and post-riding service must have been left; for the Norman landing was observed and the news transmitted 260 miles to York, where Harold received it three days afterwards, on 1 October. With the depleted ranks of his Housecarls, and such Fyrd as had either fought in the battle or had come in since, he set out for London, presumably on the 2nd, and, moving at nearly forty miles a day, reached it on the 6th. All bodies of militia met on the way would be ordered to turn about, and messages would be left for those which might arrive later. This march was a fine achievement; but its speed was not phenomenal for medieval warfare, and it is clear from passages in the Chronicles that the Housecarls, though they always fought on foot, were in effect mounted infantry, and rode horses on the march, as did also probably a proportion of the Fyrd. In London Harold remained for five full days to assemble the militia due to join there, and to allow those he had outdistanced to catch up.

It is well, at this point, to examine the Saxon and Norman armies.

The army commanded by King Harold II, the last of the Saxon kings, was composed of men of Anglian, Saxon, Jutish and Danish blood, and also, as some say, of native Danes and Welsh. It was composed of two elements, the Housecarls and the Fyrd. The Housecarls, a royal bodyguard instituted by Cnut, were professional men-at-arms who were dressed in short close-fitting leather jerkins, on which iron rings were sewn, trousers bound with thongs, and sandals. They wore their hair long, and their heads were covered by steel caps with nasal pieces and long leather flaps which fell over the shoulders. They carried pointed shields made of lime wood, which measured about 36 inches by 15 inches. Their principal weapon was the long Danish battleaxe, with which a horse and rider could be cut down at a blow; but the axe men had to be supported by swordsmen and javelin throwers, and they probably fought in combat groups like the one shown on the Bayeux Tapestry, as they were noted for their perfect drill in action. After supplying a bodyguard for the king, their chief function in battle was to stiffen the ranks of the Fyrd. The Fyrd, the old constitutional force of the country, was formed in the reign of King Alfred, and has existed as some form of militia down to the present day, the last unit being the Royal Monmouthshire Royal Engineers. The inhabitants of each five hides of land were responsible for providing one soldier for the Fyrd for two months in each year, with twenty shillings for his pay and rations. The Fyrd was dressed mostly in leather jerkins and caps, and only a few wore chain-covered shirts. Most carried a small round shield; but the supply seems to have been inadequate, for we read that shields were improvised from 'window shutters and other pieces of wood'. Their arms consisted of spears, short axes, bills, scythes, javelins, slings to hurl stones and stone-headed hammers. A very few of them were archers. They were led by thegns and their retainers. For some reason these irregular troops of the Saxon army have been represented as a rabble of ill-armed peasantry picked up at hazard, which is quite untrue. While, no doubt, the equipment and experience of the Fyrd may have left much to be desired, and made them inferior in quality to the Norman men-at-arms, they were an organized force of undoubted courage. The Bayeux Tapestry gives an erroneous impression of the appearance of the Saxon army by showing the Housecarls in Norman uniform, and the Fyrd in the dress of Norman camp followers.

The Norman military system was feudal. Each baron equipped for service a number of knights, esquires and retainers, as a condition of holding his land. These were mounted, wore mail armour or hauberks to the knees and steel helmets which gave protection to the nose. They were armed with lances swords and maces, carried kite-shaped shields, and were a skilled and disciplined force of cavalry. The infantry of the Norman army consisted of paid men-at-arms, who wore either chain shirts and iron caps, or leather jerkins and caps. They wore sandals and their legs were bound with thongs. They were armed with short axes, spears, daggers and broadswords, and their discipline was good. The archers – the artillery of the army – were armed with the short bow, which had an effective range of 100, and an extreme range of 150 yards. There were no crossbows, as they were not introduced into western Europe until later.

The strategic aspects of the campaign and the characters of the two commanders may now be considered. It is debatable whether there was any pact between William and Harald Hardrada for a simultaneous invasion, for they had met not long before; or whether Harald Hardrada forestalled William. To Harold, however, it would make no difference; for he was confronted by a two-pronged attack, and had the difficult decision to make whether to attack the Norwegians, who had actually landed, or to concentrate his forces south of London in view of the increased threat of a landing by a larger force of Normans. That he made the right decision in the circumstances is hardly open to question. On landing, William can have obtained little or no information of the whereabouts of the Saxon army until a messenger arrived from Robert son of Wymarc, a Norman who lived in the neighbourhood. This messenger is shown on the tapestry; and he brought the news of the battle of Stamford Bridge, a warning that William could not hope to defeat Harold, and the advice that he should give up his enterprise and return to Normandy. William's answer was to boast of the strength of his army, and add, 'I would fight with Harold as soon as possible.' This answer puts William's intention beyond doubt, and shows that he appreciated that the destruction of the enemy's armed forces in the field is much more important than the capture of a locality, however politically desirable that may be. This principle of war has been a fruitful source of dissension between heads of state and their military commanders in recent times; but William had the advantage of being both. His objective is clear; it was the Saxon army which, at the moment, was somewhere north of London.

Harold and William differed widely, as good generals often do, in their qualities. Harold was impetuous, bold, quick, resolute; but kind, affable and much concerned with the welfare of his followers and subjects. William was cool, careful, calculating and ruthless; but swift to take advantage of an adversary's mistake. He was a good strategist and tactician. Knowing that the longer battle was delayed the stronger Harold would become; that to seek him in the interior would mean a long campaign for which his forces were insufficient to keep open communications with the coast; and that defeat in the interior would mean annihilation, his knowledge of Harold's psychology suggested the means of achieving his object. A systematic destruction of villages in the coastal area would provide just the necessary stimulus to bring Harold down to the coast where he wanted him, with whatever troops he had with him at the moment. Once he had been decoyed within striking distance, William's intention was to deliver his blow before any more enemy troops could arrive. While this plan was being put into operation it is unlikely that he would surrender his freedom of manoeuvre by keeping his troops down by the shore at Hastings. Some position on the Baldslow Ridge, just north of Hastings, seems to be indicated, from which daily foraging and incendiary parties could be sent out. The destruction of some twenty villages around Hastings is either directly mentioned in Domesday Book, or can be deduced from the drop from pre-Conquest to post-Conquest values recorded therein. Some villages mentioned are un-identifiable and may never have been rebuilt.

Harold's plan was simple: to destroy the Norman army as he had just destroyed the Norwegians, and had defeated Gruffyth ap Llewelyn at Ruddlan in 1063, by effecting surprise through the speed of his advance. Surprise is a most potent factor in war; and the conclusion that he intended to use the same technique against William seems inescapable.

Roads have always exercised a powerful influence on stra-tegy. In 1066 the main roads of England consisted of Roman

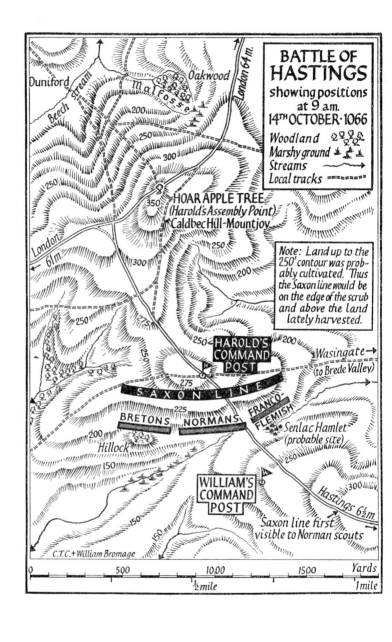

BATTLE OF
HASTINGS
showing positions
at 9 a.m.
14TH OCTOBER·1066
Woodland
Marshy ground
Streams
Local tracks

Duniford

Beech stream

Malfosse

Oakwood

London 64 m.

200

250

300

250

HOAR APPLE TREE
(Harold's Assembly Point)
Caldbec Hill-Mountjoy

350

London

61 m.

300

250

200

Note: Land up to the
250' contour was prob-
ably cultivated. Thus
the Saxon line would be
on the edge of the scrub
and above the land
lately harvested.

250

275

250

HAROLD'S
COMMAND
POST

200

Wasingate →
(to Brede Valley)

275

SAXON LINE

225

BRETONS   NORMANS

FRANCO-
FLEMISH

Senlac Hamlet
(probable site)

200

Hillock

150

250

WILLIAM'S
COMMAND
POST

Hastings 6½ m.

300

150

Saxon line first
visible to Norman scouts

150

C.T.C. + William Bromage

0   500   10.00   1500   Yards

½ mile   1 mile roads, doubtless in bad repair, and prehistoric trackways, some of which the Romans had metalled. Other ways were local tracks, unmetalled for the most part, which in Sussex were particularly founderous, and quite unsuitable for the rapid march of an army. The Roman road from Hastings to Rochester and London crossed, at Sedlescombe, the River Brede, which derives its name from its former breadth, and is known to have remained very broad and tidal at that point as late as the sixteenth century. There, in 1066, the crossing must have been made by ferry, just as travellers on Indian trunk roads have to cross rivers today. This would have rendered that portion impracticable for an army; but it could be completely avoided by taking a prehistoric trackway which ran along the ridge to the north of Hastings as far as Caldbec Hill (on the northern outskirts of Battle). There the trackway forked; and by taking the right-hand branch and passing around the source of the Brede, the Hastings–Rochester road could be regained; while by taking the left-hand branch access could be gained to the Lewes–London Roman road in the neighbourhood of Maresfield. From Harold's point of view, therefore, Caldbec Hill was a strategic point which the Norman army must pass if it marched inland; it was a nodal point of communications; it was situated at a suitable distance from Hastings to enable him to pounce on his enemy just as he had pounced on Hardrada from Tadcaster; and, in case William attacked him first, it was covered by an excellent defensive position.

Harold appointed 'The Hoar Apple Tree' as a rendezvous; and when it is learnt that the boundaries of three Hundreds met close to Caldbec Hill, and that there are fourteen known examples of apple trees having been planted at such spots, it can be said with some certainty that Caldbec Hill was the appointed rendezvous.

Caldbec Hill is only seven miles from Hastings; and the

thought that Harold was about to commit the strategic blunder of attempting to concentrate his forces within striking distance of the enemy may have been in the mind of Gyrth, his brother, when he urged him not to lead his army against William, and offered to take command himself. A much sounder plan for Harold would have been to concentrate his forces on the North Downs, where he could command both the roads by which William could advance into the interior. If William refused to be drawn into the interior, Harold, having collected all his troops, could then have advanced and crushed him with superior numbers. Harold, however, was obdurate, and marched the Saxon army out of London, presumably on 12 October, and arrived at Caldbec Hill late on the 13th. The Anglo-Saxon Chronicle remarks tersely that Harold came from the north, and fought against William before all his army had come up.

We can pass over the numerous messages, culminating in a challenge to single combat, which are said to have been exchanged between Harold and William. Whether truth or fiction they form the usual stylised prelude to a medieval account of a battle, and have no military interest.

The covering position selected by Harold, which was to become the battlefield, is a remarkable piece of ground, which, like the field of Naseby, is a watershed. From Caldbec Hill (350 feet) a neck of land, on which Battle High Street now stands, runs southwards flanked by rapidly falling ground. Just south of the abbey (275 feet) this narrow ridge dips suddenly to a height of 213 feet at the railway station approach, forming, not a valley as so many accounts state, but a saddle with a valley beginning on either side of it. Two streams, rising about 200 yards apart, flow in opposite directions down the two valleys, which must have been very marshy in 1066. At the point where the watershed begins to dip, a fairly level cross-ridge

extends from Battle Primary School on the east to the top of
the Stumblets, beyond the abbey gardens, on the west. Coming
from Hastings, the prehistoric trackway, following the watershed, ran across the saddle on a natural causeway, and climbed
the cross-ridge obliquely at about its middle. The chroniclers
describe the battle as having been fought *in planis Hastinges*,
which in medieval Latin meant *in the unwooded country* (and not
in the plains) about Hastings; from which it is easy to see how
the contracted designation battle of Hastings arose. The battlefield was in fact about one mile from the forest edge, and the
top of the ridge was probably rough untilled ground; but from
Domesday Book it can be deduced that the eastern slopes, as
also the southern slopes with land extending southward there-
from, were cultivated. The latter area was called *Santlache* and
consisted chiefly of a detached portion of the Saxon manor of
Bollington by Bulverhythe. The meaning of *Santlache* is doubtful; it may be 'sandy area'. The Norman effort to pronounce it,
or mere punning, produced *Sanguelac* and *Senlac*, meaning
'blood lake', which has achieved a certain popularity, especially in France, as a name for the battle. On this Santlache ridge
Harold formed up his troops. On no other medieval battlefield, perhaps, can the commander's post be so accurately
located; since by William's orders the high altar of the abbey
church was built on the exact spot. This place where Harold
took up his position under his two standards, the Dragon of
Wessex and the Fighting Man, is precisely where a medieval
commander might be expected to have his command post. It
was on the highest point of the ridge, about the centre of his
line, and at the point where the prehistoric trackway from the
coast was crossed by a local track called the Wasingate, which
is now represented eastwards by Marley Lane, and can still be
traced westwards as a track and avenue to Park Farm. By
forming up his troops about fifty yards in front of his command

post, they would have their backs to the rising ground, and he, looking over their heads, could see what the enemy was doing. By resting the right flank about 150 yards to the west of the present abbey terrace, and the left about 50 yards south of the primary school, a position 800 yards long and level for the most part was secured, while the ground fell away from both flanks. Many writers have suggested that the flanks were refused, that is bent back; but the result of this would have been to place some men on lower ground, and so throw away the great advantage of the position, namely the difficulty of attacking it with cavalry. Moreover, to refuse the flanks at all was really unnecessary because medieval attacks on a flank were usually frontal. Besides the two streams mentioned, which caused substantial obstacles across the front of the position, six or more other streams rise behind the cross-ridge, and run in small deep hollows which made the flanks and rear difficult of access. From every point of view the position must have been ideal for an army of footsoldiers to hold against an enemy strong in cavalry and archers. Harold had visited the south coast the previous summer, and there can be little doubt that he reconnoitred at leisure the Santlache ridge for possible use should the Normans land in that sector; just as Wellington reconnoitred the ridge of Mont St Jean a long time before the battle of Waterloo. The question whether the Saxons were able to construct any artificial obstacle in front of their line has been a subject of controversy. While it is just possible that a *cheval de frise* of stakes cut and carried on the march could have been erected as some slight protection, it is clear that time did not permit the construction of any solid obstacles; and it is difficult to understand why the fantastic story of the poet Wace, that a sort of castle of tree trunks surrounded by a ditch was built on the ridge, was ever believed at all.

From the descriptions given, the Saxon dispositions appear

to have resembled a Macedonian phalanx. From the estimated numbers it could have been nine or ten ranks deep, of which the front rank would consist of Housecarls and the remainder of Fyrd. A strong detachment of Housecarls guarded the king. A constantly recurring phrase in descriptions of the battle is 'the shield wall'; and some writers have asserted that the shields were 'locked'. The suggestion conveyed is that shields could, in some manner, confer on a battle line additional power to resist shock. This is a misconception of the functions of a shield, which were to stop or deflect arrows and other missiles, and to protect the soldier from sword-cuts in hand-to-hand combat. Against charging horsemen and their lances, shields would be useless; nor could a Housecarl have wielded his battleaxe at the critical moment if helping to form a shield wall. Shield walls were formed as a protection against arrows and other missiles; and to do this the Housecarls, owing to the narrowness of their shields, had to stand sideways as shown on the tapestry. When it came to close combat a shield wall had of necessity to be broken up.

To give a trustworthy estimate of the number of troops brought to the battlefield is difficult. General James, as already stated, estimated that 11,000 men were conveyed across the Channel, but when due allowance has been made for sailors, sutlers, camp followers, garrisons left at Pevensey and Hastings, and sick, it is doubtful if more than 8,000 men of William's army reached the field. On the Saxon side, there are no figures of any value on which an estimate can be based, so the problem must be attacked in another way. The conflict lasted eight hours, which is nearly three times the average length of a battle in those days, and points to almost perfect equality, in the aggregate, of morale, training, weapons and numbers. Between the commanders there was little to choose. Morale must have been exceptionally high on both sides; on the Norman side

H

because the expedition was in the nature of a crusade which the pope had blessed, the Channel had been crossed and rich manors for all lay round the corner; and on the Saxon side because they were fighting for their Motherland under their elected king, had just destroyed the Norwegian invaders and were confidently expecting to destroy the Normans in the same way. Again there is little to choose. The excellence of the Housecarls, the finest troops in the field, may be set against the inferiority of the Fyrd. The argument, so often advanced, that the Saxon method of fighting entirely on foot was out-of-date, can be met by pointing out that the terrain put the Norman cavalry at a considerable disadvantage. There remains the question of numbers. The inferiority of the Fyrd might be redressed, perhaps, by about 800 extra men; so that if 8,000 is accepted as the Norman strength, that of the Saxons might be put at 8,800, to which must be added any fyrdmen who arrived during the battle. These two figures are in fact in agreement with the average of the estimates of eleven writers on the battle.

On the Norman side, William, having heard of the approach of the Saxon army through the forest, presumably from scouts, recalled his troops from their scattered billets and ordered a stand-to-arms. It is one of the literary devices of medieval chroniclers to assert that on the night before the battle nobody slept; the chronicler's own side spent the night in religious devotion, while the enemy spent it in revelry. This fiction appears at its best in accounts of the battle of Hastings; though the men of Harold's army who were at Stamford Bridge had covered 260 miles in seven marching days, while others had come from as far afield as Somersetshire. They at least, except for some sentries, must have slept like logs.

Dawn broke on 14 October at about 5.30 am with the waning moon (twenty-two days old) still high in the sky; and it is recorded that the morning was unusually light for the time of year; so that the head of the Norman column could have begun its march about 6 am and reached *Hecheland* in an hour if, as supposed, their bivouac was on the Baldslow ridge. *Hecheland*, meaning heathland, has been identified with the hilltop marked 462 on the Hastings–Battle road, really the summit of Telham Hill, but now called Blackhorse Hill. A high mound marks the spot. It is known to have been erected less than 200 years ago; but it is tempting to think that it may cover the *tertre* from which William addressed his troops. Here a knight called Vital, a vassal of Bishop Odo, William's half-brother, who had been out scouting, reported that he had sighted the Saxon army. The tapestry records that Harold received similar information about the Norman army at about the same time. The duke ordered the column to halt and chain-armour was donned. He presumably gave orders to his sub-ordinate commanders; but a speech to his whole army, such as the chroniclers pretend, was clearly impossible. Owing to the gentle declivity of Telham Hill, the Norman army and the Saxons on the Santlache ridge were not mutually visible until the former had reached the 300 feet contour, and the two forces were separated by a bare half-mile. About 8 am the head of the Norman column would reach the saddle between the two streams already mentioned, which is now crossed by the Hastings road between the Senlac Hotel and the lodge of the abbey park. How to deploy his army must have presented William with a problem. Deployment short of the saddle, and a subsequent march in line, would have been precluded by the broken ground and marshy valleys; while deployment after crossing the saddle would entail flank marches almost within archery range of the enemy. Considering that Harold would not abandon his strong position to attack him during the move-ment, William decided to deploy after crossing the saddle along a line little more than 150 yards from the enemy, and about 50 feet lower.

The army of the Duke William comprised three divisions, of which the Breton division, under the command of Alan Fergant of Britanny, was leading the column. We are told that it was stronger than the Franco-Flemish division, and its strength may be estimated at about 2,100. Owing to the slanting approach of the trackway it needed only a slight change of direction to bring it opposite the right flank of the Saxon position, where it formed up in front of the hillock which is shown on the tapestry, and which still forms a prominent feature of the battlefield. It thus faced the only part of the ridge which is still approximately in its original state, namely that to the west of the abbey gardens; and also perhaps a little of the terrace. The Franco-Flemish division, estimated strength 1,600 under Roger of Montgomerie, second in the column, had to execute a sharp right wheel to take up its position opposite the Saxon left wing, which can now be identified as the part of the ridge which runs from the Hastings road to the primary school. Its forming-up line is now covered by the omnibus depot and adjoining buildings and gardens. The Norman division, said to be stronger than the other two combined, may be estimated at about 4,300. It was under the personal command of the duke, with whom were his two half-brothers, Robert Count of Mortain, and Odo bishop of Bayeux. When the other two divisions had deployed to the left and right, it deployed to its front and filled the gap between them. The duke's command post was on a hill exactly opposite that of Harold. Examination of the railway cutting just west of the bridge discloses that it was cut through a knoll, which would have provided the only place which could at all have fitted the description. There, presumably, the duke, under the papal banner, and the two leopards of Normandy, watched the opening phases of the battle. The three divisions formed up in three similar columns: archers in front, men-at-arms next, and the cavalry, which General James estimates as just under 30 per cent of the entire force, in rear. This formation suggests that William's tactical plan envisaged three phases: first phase, a shot of arrows, equivalent in those days to artillery preparation; second phase, assault by heavy infantry to effect breaches; third phase, exploitation of the breaches, and pursuit by the cavalry. Of the march discipline and march formation of the Normans nothing is known; but if they resembled in any way that of modern troops, the column was about three miles long, and consequently took an hour to form up in line; bringing the time to 9 am which, on 14 October Old Style, which is 20 October New Style, would be the third hour as stated by the chroniclers. The trumpets then sounded and the battle began.

Advancing in open order to within a hundred yards of the Saxon line (the effective range of the short bow), the archers stuck their large quivers in the ground, as shown on the tapestry, and began to shoot. Shooting uphill, the low arrows would be taken on the shields of the Housecarls, while the high ones would pass over the heads of the whole Saxon phalanx. Due to lack of Saxon archers there was hardly any reply; and for this very reason the Norman archers soon ran out of arrows; for normally the enemy's arrows were relied upon to keep up the ammunition supply.

The shot of arrows having failed to have any appreciable effect, the second phase began. The heavy infantry advancing up the slope were met by a storm of missiles of every sort, which has been described as quite unprecedented. Even the archers, who kept their distance, are reported to have suffered casualties. The Housecarls maintained their rigid line, and the Normans on closing with them suffered severely because their shields and mail were not proof against the Saxon weapons, notably the battleaxe, against which adequate protection would be impossible. The Bretons, advancing up the easy slopes of the western sector, would be the first to meet with this murderous reception. Unsupported for the moment on their right, they could make no headway, were thrown into confusion, and fell back in disorder, carrying their cavalry with them, into the marshy bottom of the valley, where the cavalry got bogged and heavy casualties were suffered. The Fyrd, we are told, pursued the Bretons down the slope; and whether, as is usually assumed, they disobeyed their orders by doing so, will be discussed later. In modern as in ancient warfare, when a flank is overwhelmed, the neighbouring troops tend to fall back in succession to conform. Owing to the flight of the Bretons, the Norman division, unsupported on its left, fell back, and the retrograde movement spread along the line and involved the Franco-Flemish division on the extreme right. Even the baggage guard was affected, and the whole army of the duke was disorganized and in danger of rout. Seeing from his command post the serious situation which had developed, William galloped down into the mêlée to restore the situation. In the general confusion the rumour circulated that he had been killed. Dashing into the midst of the fugitives, he pushed back his helmet and shouted that he was still alive. Then, assisted by Bishop Odo and Eustace of Boulogne, he succeeded in stopping the panic. After some confused fighting he launched some cavalry of the Norman division which, well placed to charge downhill against the flank of the Saxons who were pursuing the Bretons, struck them between the hillock and the marsh. Some managed to regain their lines, others climbed on to the hillock, but the majority were destroyed. (See plate 5b.)

Soldiers cannot fight hand-to-hand for eight hours on end; and there must have been pauses in the conflict, although they are not recorded by the chroniclers. A long interlude must have occurred after the events just described. The Normans had to reform, the Saxons to fill their gaps and on both sides missiles had to be recovered and redistributed. The opportunity would be taken to consume any food or drink available.

The significance of the critical events of the second phase of the battle can now be assessed. The sudden sortie of the Norman army from Hastings forced Harold to meet the blow by occupying Santlache ridge, the position he had chosen to cover his concentration. That he should suddenly be forced to assume a defensive role was, in the circumstances, unavoidable. It was a situation which frequently arises in the thrust and parry of warfare. What is difficult to understand is why it has been almost universally supposed that Harold's plan for fighting the battle was the sterile one of a purely passive defence. His previous exploits had shown him to be an aggressive leader, thoroughly imbued with the offensive spirit, a Rommel of his time. Such a plan would not accord with his character; and to suppose that he never contemplated any counter-attack at all, does scant justice to his skill as a military commander. If this is accepted, was he able to deliver his planned counterattack or not?

In the episode of the retreat of the Bretons, one cannot fail to notice the very strange disproportion between the alleged cause and the recorded effect. A supposed undisciplined rush of some Fyrd caused such widespread disorganization of the whole Norman army that their own chroniclers admit that it was little short of a *débâcle*. The episode receives detailed treatment on the Bayeux Tapestry, which includes the death of Gyrth and Leofwin, the king's brothers, who, one supposes, would almost certainly lead a main counter-attack. The moment for delivering a counter-attack is when the enemy has spent the main force of his attack. If this episode was a counter-attack, the impetuous Harold did not wait for that moment, and thereby committed a tactical error. Finally, there is the negative evidence that he did not attack the Normans when they were in a state of confusion, for which some historians have blamed him. If however that confusion was the result of a Saxon counter-attack, it is easy to understand why Harold was unable to make any further effort. It is here suggested that this episode of the battle was, in fact, Harold's planned counter-attack, which was delivered much too soon, and was met and crushed, though with some difficulty, by the duke's prompt action.

William had now to decide what to do next, as the first two phases had not gone at all according to plan. For the third phase, his decision was the hazardous one of launching his knights and their followers, his corps d'élite, against the unbroken Saxon line, much as Napoleon, over 700 years later, launched his cavalry against the British squares at Waterloo. The result was not dissimilar: bodies of knights climbed up the ridge until the storm of missiles which had assailed the infantry broke upon them. There could have been no momentum such as is imparted by a charge, and all they could have done was to force their frightened and jibbing horses close enough to the Saxon line to prod at it with their lances, while the Housecarls cut down those they could reach with their Danish battleaxes. This unequal contest, in which the flower of the Norman army sustained heavy casualties, must have lasted some time. At length the cavalry of the Norman division, about the centre, were falling back exhausted when the Saxons issued from their lines and pursued them.

It may have been a local counter-attack, or the Fyrd may have got out of hand, but the Norman cavalry fled before them. Before the Saxons could regain their lines the duke launched another cavalry charge which fell upon their flank and effected great slaughter. Once again an awkward situation had been saved by the duke's prompt action. Two similar incidents are said to have occurred on the Franco-Flemish front, and to have been dealt with in the same way. As a result of the losses sustained by the Saxons in these sorties, parts of their line became so weakened that it became necessary for them to draw in the flanks, and concentrate more closely about the standard.

As most of the accounts of the battle give such prominence to the first of the incidents just described, stating that the Norman retreat was a stratagem designed to draw the Saxons out of their line, and that *the same troops* wheeled about and charged their pursuers, it is necessary to assess the credibility of that story. A 'feigned retreat', it is claimed, was a recognized tactical operation in ancient warfare, which has been mentioned by many chroniclers as having occurred in many battles. In view of the disbelief with which a 'retreat according to plan' in an enemy communiqué during the last wars was received, would it not be more correct to say that a 'feigned retreat' was the recognized method by which chroniclers concealed the fact that the troops on their own side had run away?

A 'feigned retreat' would demand that every man taking part in it had to know when to retreat, how far to retreat and when to turn round and fight back; and, moreover, that these movements had to be carefully synchronized, or disaster would result. To arrange this in the heat of battle with men fighting hand-to-hand for their lives was clearly impossible. Could the operation have been a carefully rehearsed act, set off, perhaps, by a trumpet call? Similar acts, performed at military tournaments and tattoos with the well-drilled and disciplined soldiers of to-day need much rehearsal and, even with the small numbers employed, are difficult enough to stage. Is it possible that a feudal force at the beginning of this millennium could have performed such an act at all? Finally, there is the military maxim, evolved after long years of experience in warfare, that 'troops committed to the attack cannot be made to change their direction'. If the situation created by the real flight of some troops was restored by an immediate charge of fresh troops, the result would be much the same as if a 'feigned retreat' had been possible and had taken place, as far as the progress of the battle was concerned. A 'feigned retreat', therefore, the chroniclers made it, in order to save the face of the troops who ran away.

Up to this point William had used his archers, infantry and cavalry independently; and none had achieved a decisive result. Now, owing perhaps to diminished numbers rather than to an early attempt at co-operation, he employed them simultaneously. The attacking force for this, the fourth and final phase of the battle for the Santlache ridge, is likely to have consisted of mixed elements of infantry and cavalry; numbers of the latter having, perforce, to fight on foot because of the great loss of horses which must have occurred in the third phase. The archers, having drawn fresh arrows from munition wagons like the one shown on the tapestry, gave support to the attack by an overhead shot. One of the arrows of this barrage wounded Harold in the eye. A report spread that the king had fallen, which caused confusion among the Fyrd. Mounted Norman cavalry, riding up the easier western slope of the ridge, gained the top probably about 3 pm, and so were able, by charging along it, to roll up the disintegrating Saxon line. William himself, having scaled the hill, saw that the Saxon left was also greatly weakened and sent an urgent order to the Franco-Flemish division to detach some troops to assist on that flank. In response, Eustace of Boulogne hastily collected a small force, led it to the end of the ridge and attacked from the east. The hard core of the Saxon line, containing the king's headquarters, was now invested from both sides; but the Housecarls which composed it, a constantly diminishing number, fought doggedly on. Eventually so many had fallen that a party of knights comprising Guy of Ponthieu, Giffard, Montfort and Eustace of Boulogne was able to reach Harold, whom they cut down and killed on the spot where, within ten years of the battle, the high altar of the abbey church was erected. The struggle on the ridge had gone on for two hours, and the sun was setting while the remnants of the Housecarls, preserving their discipline even in this extremity, were still offering resistance in small bodies. But the Fyrd had fled 'some on horseback, some on foot, some taking to the roads, most by bye-paths' to quote from William of Poitiers. Eventually such Housecarls as remained alive retreated to the forest. Saxon resistance, however, had not yet ceased. An anonymous warrior appears either to have rallied the remnants of the Housecarls, or, alternatively, to have been in command of some Fyrd that had just arrived. Realizing perhaps from fugitives that the main position had been lost, he occupied with them a rearguard position which is described as being associated with a steep bank, many ditches, a kind of ancient causeway and a long ravine overgrown with bushes and brambles, to which later the name *Malfosse* (Evil Ditch) was given. The name Malfosse has been lost in modern times, and for the last hundred years there has been discussion about its location. A recent thorough piece of local research has proved from Battle Abbey deeds, which are now in America, that in 1240 and 1279 the locality of Oak Wood was actually called *Maufosse*, which is merely a later variant of *Malfosse*, and that a farm track then crossed the Evil Ditch at the same spot as the modern road. The Malfosse is situated one mile from the battlefield where a high causeway carries the modern London road over a watercourse in a hollow which runs down from Oak Wood which is 200 yards to the east. The hollow is now much silted up, but has the appearance of former depth and still has steepness of sides. On the top of the higher northern bank is a flat piece of ground nearly 400 yards long, eminently suitable to hold as a rearguard position. Its right is secured by a steep scarp falling 30 feet to a stream, while its left rests on a fanlike pattern of small streams, all of which fits the description 'steep bank' and 'many ditches'. A formidable obstacle along the whole front of the position would have been furnished by the Malfosse in its original state. Such a suitable small defensive position could hardly have been found in a moment during the headlong flight of a beaten army, particularly as it did not lie astride the road which fugitives would be likely to take. The unknown commander, it must seem, had sufficient time to reconnoitre it deliberately, which serves to show that medieval military operations were not always as haphazard as they are often represented to have been.

The chroniclers' accounts are now clearer, and from them we may reconstruct what happened at the Malfosse. As the battle on the Santlache ridge ended, the duke ordered an immediate pursuit. 'It was evening, already the hinge was turning the day towards the shades,' wrote a chronicler; whence we may infer that the sun was setting, which it did on that day at five o'clock, and that there was about one hour of daylight left. As the Norman cavalry was galloping down the gentle slope to the north of Caldbec Hill, the leading horsemen came suddenly to the grass-covered edge of the ravine. Unable to hold their horses, they plunged into it followed by those in rear 'killing one another as they fell suddenly and without warning one on the top of the other'. Others, attempting to cross the obstacle by the ancient and presumably dilapidated causeway, fell off it and added to the shambles. From their elevated position on the opposite bank the Saxon rearguard assailed them with all kinds of missiles. Eustace of Boulogne, at the head of fifty horsemen, saw what had happened and turned back. In doing so he met the duke who, with a broken lance in his hand, had ridden up close enough to assess the situation. Eustace told the duke that it was death to go on, but the duke sternly ordered him to do so. At that moment Eustace was struck down by a battleaxe, presumably wielded by some Housecarl who had contrived to creep up unobserved. Eustace, only wounded, was carried away and the duke then took charge of operations and 'disdaining any fear or disgrace advanced and crushed his opponents'. Looking at the ground, the only way to capture the position with cavalry would seem to be by turning its left flank by a wide detour round the 'many ditches'. We are told that 'in this action several noble Normans fell, their courage being hampered by the precipitous character of the country. Thus the victory was consummated and he [the duke] returned to the battlefield.' By then it must have been quite dark, and there could have been no further pursuit, for the 'hunters' moon did not rise until about midnight.

It was the custom of the armies of Charlemagne, whom William admired, to build a cairn of stones called a *mountjoy* to commemorate a victory; and the duke must have caused one to be erected on Caldbec Hill, for the locality has been continuously called Mountjoy to this day.

So ended the most famous and important battle ever fought in England, and one of the decisive battles of the world. Why did our Norman ancestors win, and our Saxon ancestors lose this conflict? It has been ascribed to the inferiority of the Saxons in weapons, and their out-of-date method of warfare, but that does not get to the root of the matter. In fighting power the two armies, as has been explained, showed themselves to be practically equal. The commanders were probably the greatest captains of war of their period, and their skill also equal; but just as an expert chess player can win a game from an equally skilful opponent, so William in the battle of Hastings appears to have out-generalled Harold. Having induced him to commit the strategic error of attempting to complete his concentration at Caldbec Hill within striking distance of his enemy, William struck immediately, and thus threw him on the defensive, for which he was unprepared and temperamentally unsuited. Reasons have been given for supposing that Harold counter-attacked prematurely in the second phase, a tactical error. If he had not committed the first error he would have stood a good chance of defeating the Normans on another field, while if he had not committed the second he might even have defeated them on the Santlache ridge. As it was, the issue hung in the balance, and the Normans were nearly driven from the field once, and put to flight locally three times before the end came. One cannot but admire the tactical ability of William, whose lightning cavalry charges restored the situation each time, until the balance tipped in his favour. If it had tipped the other way, English history would have been very different.

The next day, 15 October, was devoted, we are told, to the burial of the dead. The Normans were buried; but William of Poitiers, after an uncharitable outburst that the enemy did not deserve Christian burial, states that William graciously allowed Saxon families to take away their dead. As this could only have affected a few local soldiers, we may suppose that the majority of corpses were left on the field, as at Stamford Bridge, where Orderic records that he saw heaps of bones seventy years later. The sub-soil of the Battle district is acid and, as far as is known, no authentic grave pits have ever been discovered. Of Harold's own burial reports are conflicting. William ordered that he should be buried upon the seashore; but this was either never carried out, or his remains were removed later; for there is little doubt that his final resting place was Waltham Abbey.

Next day, 16 October, William returned to Hastings, his army presumably being again scattered for subsistence. Thus it remained for five nights. We can recognize here the practical need for rest and reorganization, for it had been badly mauled.

It is now necessary to estimate the number of William's troops who survived the battle. Let us take two sanguinary modern hand-to-hand engagements of which we have details of casualties – the assault of Badajoz, and the charge of the Heavy Brigade at Balaclava. In the former, casualties were 37 per cent, and in the latter 26 per cent. Setting the use of firearms at Badajoz against the long duration of the battle of Hastings, and the lack of armour in both the modern engagements against the use of armour at Hastings, the percentage of casualties should lie somewhere between these two figures. At the risk of making it too high, we may, perhaps, place it at 30 per cent. We are told that a garrison was left at Hastings. Allowing 200 infantry for this, and adhering to the previous estimate of troops brought to the battle, we may estimate the number of troops available for the march into the interior at 1,680 cavalry and 3,720 infantry, a total of 5,400 men.

William had now to form a plan for dealing with a situation which always confronts an invading commander when he has defeated the enemy's main army. The capital has to be occupied, centres of potential resistance captured and attempts to carry on the war by re-formed bodies of troops or bands of guerrillas crushed. In this case there were in effect three capital cities to be dealt with: Winchester the ancient capital and still the seat of the Treasury, London the chief commercial city and place where the national parliament of notables was in session at the moment, and Canterbury the ecclesiastical capital. William had also received warning that a large force was assembling at Dover. His plan, therefore, was to secure the surrender of these towns, if possible, by demonstrations of force, if not, by siege and assault. Dover and Canterbury, the two nearest towns, naturally came first on the list.

The chroniclers' accounts of the Norman army's movements in carrying out William's plan are so meagre that recourse must be had to some other source of information on which to base reasoned conjecture as to what actually occurred. Such is provided by the research, in 1900, of the Hon. F. H. Baring, who noticed that in south-eastern England the value, as recorded in Domesday Book, when a Norman owner took over a manor was in many cases more than 20 per cent lower than that recorded at the death of King Edward. Considering that there must be some special reason for this, he plotted 217 of such places, and found that they occurred along possible lines of march of the Norman army. He deduced a main route from Hastings to Dover, Canterbury and along the Pilgrims' Way to Winchester, with offshoots to Southwark and West Middlesex. He traced the landing of reinforcements at Fareham; and two columns which, after taking a large and a small sweep, crossed the Thames at Wallingford and Goring. He saw the main body advancing up the Icknield Way and then fanning out as far as the River Ouse, and Trumpington near Cambridge. He reached the conclusion that *Little* and not *Great* Berkhampsted was the place where William received the surrender of London, at the head of a force dispersed in an inverted triangle behind him. He also hinted that it might be possible to estimate the number of troops from his figures. While we can agree with Baring that his plot does, in fact, show the passage of Norman troops and to some extent the relative numbers which visited different localities, it reveals little of any military plan, or the actual strengths of the Norman detachments.

To obtain more detailed information from Baring's figures, a yardstick must be found. Inspection of Baring's list of 217 manors discloses the remarkable fact that no less than 110 of them suffered a spoliation of £4 to £7. Let us call this spoliation

5a. 'Horses being landed at Pevensey': from *The Bayeux Tapestry*, edited by Sir Frank Stenton (Phaidon Press). See p. 90.

5b. 'Saxonfyrd holding a hill': from *The Bayeux Tapestry*, edited by Sir Frank Stenton (Phaidon Press). See p. 104.

6a. The hillock today. (See p. 104.)

6b. The Malfosse today, at the London road crossing. (See p. 111.)

A. Other groups are B, of 36 manors at £8 to £11; C, of 23 manors at £12 to £16; and D, of 12 manors at £18 to £22. Another group of 27 manors which can be called P (patrol), suffered a small spoliation of £2 to £3, and the remaining nine, which can be labelled L (large), show a spoliation of £25 to £80. When plotted, the groups A, C and D stand out with startling distinctness with A towering above the rest. Further inspection shows that A, with its average value of £5/6s. is the yardstick or 'Spoliation Unit' we seek; for C is almost exactly twice, and D nearly three times A. P can be fitted in as half a unit and B as one and a half. L spoliations vary and must be treated individually as they occur.

The next step is to plot Baring's 217 manors, and attach to each its spoliation letter. Two more facts emerge; the first that, except in an area north of London, the spoliated manors fall into clusters; and the second that the clusters occur at intervals of approximately twenty-five miles. The following deductions may now be made:

1. That A represents the spoliation suffered by the stay of a normal unit of the Norman army for a minimum period.

2. That a cluster of spoliations represents the halting area of a force.

3. That the usual length of march was about twenty-five miles.

As regards the minimum period, the necessity for catching, killing, dressing, cooking and eating animals, also for collecting corn for grinding and making bread, would make daily marching impossible, and the minimum period can be considered as two nights. The value in spoliation units of each cluster gives a means of identification of bodies of troops. Thus clusters of the same value occurring at intervals of twenty-five miles along

I

a road or track indicates not only the march of a column but also its relative strength.

The first halt of the army when it left the Hastings area was to an area including Lympne and Folkestone, where there are $23\frac{1}{2}$ (say 24) units of spoliation. This provides a means of assessing the strength of Norman army units; for this spoliation was caused by 1,680 cavalry and 3,720 infantry. If we assume that each cavalryman with his horse caused one and a half times as much spoliation as an infantryman, the strength of the cavalry unit works out at 168 and the infantry unit at 260. These are awkward figures; but they point in a rough way to a squadron of 150 men and a company of 250, and the army is seen to consist of 10 squadrons and 14 companies.

The location of the first halt raises the question of where the march began, Hastings itself being too far away. On the road, and twenty-five miles from the halt, is Northiam which suffered total devastation, though unconnected with the strategic devastations before the battle. William would naturally want to review his troops after the battle, before beginning further operations; so it is suggested that he assembled them at Northiam for this purpose on 21 October.

What follows is a reconstruction of the final phase of William's campaign of 1066, based upon the narratives of the chroniclers, the extension of Baring's theory just enunciated and what the late Lieut-Colonel Burne called 'Inherent Military Probability'.

On 22 October the Norman army marched from Northiam to Folkestone, where a cavalry screen of six squadrons was thrown out to block the Roman road to Canterbury and the ancient trackway inland. On the march, two squadrons were detached at Tenterden to carry out a reprisal on Romney for the murder of the occupants of the ship which was blown ashore there at the crossing. They rejoined later by a road across the marsh.

On 24 October the army moved to an area astride the Roman roads north-west of Dover. The town and fortress surrendered unexpectedly to the threat. Here William remained a week to improve the defences of the castle, during which time an epidemic suddenly struck the army and caused some deaths. Usually ascribed to dysentery, it may from the evidence, according to a recent medical opinion, have been gastro-enteritis due to contaminated food or water, or both. About one-third of the army, some 1,700 men, did not take part in the next marches.

On 31 October, leaving a garrison of one company of in-fantry and all the sick at Dover, the army moved to both sides of Canterbury, but the city had already submitted.

William had easily secured two of his objectives and now formed a plan for capturing the other two. London could not be besieged from the south, but a demonstration of force might bring about its surrender. We are told he sent 500 cavalry to Southwark for this purpose; and $3\frac{1}{2}$ spoliation units at Camberwell strikingly confirm this. A supporting force of two companies of infantry marched to Battersea in two stages.

At the same time orders were issued for eight squadrons of cavalry and five companies of infantry to assemble on the Pilgrims' Way about Nutfield in Surrey, for the march to Winchester. William himself, while these moves were in progress, went to the 'Broken Tower', where he suffered a belated though not severe attack of sickness. This place may have been at Sevenoaks, where he would be well placed to pro-ceed either to London or Winchester as circumstances might demand.

London failed to surrender; and the cavalry, after burning Southwark, joined the Winchester force at Nutfield. The surplus infantry crossed the Thames by Hampton ford, left posts at the river crossings and marched to West Middlesex about Hayes, where they were joined later by the convalescents whose short marches are observable. This force may have been ordered to collect materials for siege works; for in December it occupied Westminster and threatened siege operations against London from the west.

On or about 6 November the Winchester force marched along the Pilgrims' Way, the cavalry to Farnham and the infantry to Albury, and on the 8th continued to areas north of Winchester, and about South Warnborough respectively.

A reinforcement of three cavalry squadrons had landed at Fareham at the end of October, and was in the Meon valley. It was ordered to form a flank guard for the forthcoming northward march, and take up positions about the Roman road and West Ridgeway knot of communications near Andover.

Winchester surrendered to the threat, together with Queen Edith, widow of King Edward and sister of Harold. After a stay of four nights the force, covered by its flank guard, marched northward to the Thames crossings, the cavalry to Wallingford, the crossing place of the Icknield Way, and the infantry to Goring, crossing place of the West Ridgeway. Some time was spent about Wallingford, notably in the Sutton Courtney area, and at a camp pitched at Crowmarsh. Wallingford was an important place; the barracks of the Housecarls, occupying fifteen acres, were there; and the eleventh-century Norman motte may well have been erected at the time under William's direction. At Wallingford, Stigand, archbishop of Canterbury, came in and made his submission to William.

At the beginning of the fourth week in November, the force marched along the Icknield Way to the Aston Clinton neighbourhood. The flank guard, after holding the river line about Faringdon, became a rearguard and fell back to guard the crossings from Dorchester to Goring. On arrival at Aston Clinton, the campaign assumes a different form. London had not yet submitted and might have to be besieged. An area had been entered across which several Roman roads converged on London. William had shown himself apprehensive of interference from the south-west, but not from the west or north-west. Now he was apprehensive of enemy forces, probably those of Edwin and Morcar, coming from the north. He did not realize, perhaps, the extent of their defeat at Fulford.

To obtain early warning of an enemy approach from the north, William threw a line of observation posts across the Roman roads at a distance of fifty miles from London, from Trumpington near Cambridge to near St Neots, and thence along the River Ouse to the neighbourhood of Stony Stratford. About ten miles back from this line a support line through Ampthill was established along roads now recognized as Roman, and numbered by archaeologists 176 and 23a.

London in 1066 had probably no more than 25,000 inhabitants. It was contained within the Roman walls, in the square mile known to-day as the City. We know that there was a small suburb at Southwark, and there may have been others just outside the walls at Bishopsgate, Cripplegate and Ludgate. Between London and Westminster there was two miles of open country.

Having posted the observation lines, William can now have had at his disposal little more than 3,500 men for the investment of London.

Of these some 1,500 would be required to stage the siege operation. These troops, brought up from Hayes, established themselves at Westminster and began their task. Meanwhile, Hertingfordbury is indicated as William's headquarters, where, with the remainder of his forces all within eight miles to the north of him, he awaited events. It was early in December.

The threat of siege and assault was sufficient; a deputation of bishops and other notables came out to meet William at Little Berkhampsted, a village two miles from Hertingfordbury. The composition of this deputation is uncertain; the only persons on whom the chroniclers agree being Edgar the Atheling, who had been elected king, and Ealdred, archbishop of York. These gave the city into his power, brought to him all the hostages he demanded and jointly asked him to take the crown. The Conqueror did not immediately accept the crown, as he was not in possession of the whole of England, but finally agreed to do so on the advice of his officers.

He would not enter London until a detachment had constructed a Norman motte of the usual type in the south-east corner of the Roman wall. This work is supposed to have been on the site of the White Tower at the Tower of London.

While awaiting coronation, the Norman chroniclers state, things were so peaceful that William might have gone hawking; but the English chroniclers complain that he allowed his troops to harry the country and burn towns. They certainly set fire to Dover, Southwark and Westminster, but in general there is no evidence of wanton spoliation away from the line of march.

William proceeded to London by the recently rediscovered Roman road from Stevenage, and entered the city by Cripplegate.

He was crowned king of England by Archbishop Ealdred in Westminster Abbey on Christmas Day 1066; and his descendant in the twenty-ninth generation, who is also descended from the Saxon kings, sits on the throne to-day.

IV · The Effects of the Norman Conquest

by FRANK BARLOW

Professor of History, University of Exeter

The longest, most elaborate and most detailed account of the Conquest is E. A. Freeman's *The History of the Norman Conquest, Its Causes and Its Results*, published in six large quarto volumes between 1867 and 1879, and containing well over a million words. General Patton perused it before D-day in 1944, ostensibly to find out which roads William had used in Normandy and Brittany, although possibly as a soporific; but it is now not much read. Nevertheless its influence has been profound.

Freeman believed in the fundamental continuity of English history from Æthelberht to Albert, and in his book started with the Germanic settlements in Britain in the fifth century, and finished with 'the emergence of a national state' under Edward I. He asserted, 'The great truth . . . that the importance of the Norman conquest is not the importance either of a beginning or of an ending, but the importance of a turning point.' He believed that the Conquest did no more than give a twist to the gradual elaboration of political institutions implicit in primitive Germanic society. He did not regard the Conquest – at least in the long view – as harmful. It taught the English to know themselves, to refine their virtues and enabled them to re-emerge and collaborate with a noble king in establishing parliamentary government. Freeman wrote, 'The fiery trial which England went through was a fire which did not destroy, but only purified. She came forth once more the England of old. She came forth with her ancient laws formed into shapes better suited to changed times, and with a new body of fellow workers in those long-estranged kinsmen whom birth on her soil had changed into kinsmen again.'

One scholar, however, was not impressed. J. H. Round, working in a much narrower field, primarily that of genealogy and local history, and irritated by the great assumptions and inaccurate detail, the haziness at critical points and, perhaps, the arrogant tediousness of Freeman's vast canvas, offered a cataclysmic view of the Conquest which found favour for a time. He disliked what little he knew of Old-English history, was authoritarian in politics and had the 'snob-values' of the genealogist and antiquarian. For him it was inconceivable that England's virtues could have sprung from that Germanic morass. 'There must be, surely,' he wrote, 'an instinctive feeling that in England our consecutive political history does, in a sense, begin with the Norman conquest.' This protest against nineteenth-century evolutionary views had its effect and a generation of scholars backed Round against Freeman. There was, they maintained, a real and profound break in the continuity of English history. The origin of many, if not most, medieval English governmental and social institutions must be sought in Normandy and France and not in the Old-English kingdom.

Yet historical opinion has veered again. Round's attack, although devastating, was on a narrow front. It was possible to re-form the line. To-day, once more, students of English kingship and government, of the English church and of English economic history will assume at least basic continuity from the Old-English to the Anglo-Norman kingdom, and will look to the Norman duchy mainly for the influences that in the later eleventh century modified the indigenous pattern. Moreover, they will distinguish between the purely Norman contribution and those ideas and fashions whose entry was simply facilitated by the Conquest. The Normans not only brought in foreign wares but remained active carriers of them.

Also there has been a tendency among historians to recover Freeman's width of vision, his ability to see England as part of Europe and Christendom, and Normandy within the framework of the Frankish kingdom. Differences in their institutions and cultures are now often regarded as variations within a common sociological system. Such a view permits intricate and delicate inter-reactions to occur when different regional and national customs are brought together.

The historian's position, however, is not exactly as it was. Incessant research in a subject which has continued to hold the interest of scholars, has produced a knowledge and understanding of the Old-English kingdom, the duchy of Normandy and the Anglo-Norman kingdom far more exact in detail than was possible in Freeman's day. Some problems have been re-examined time after time, most fruitfully when there has been a true appreciation of current European scholarship. English history cannot usefully be studied outside its context. Hence, although there is still much conflict of view, and still room for the individual interpretation, the factual basis is firmer and the scale of disagreement has diminished.

Norman apologists, like William of Poitiers, the duke's panegyrist, maintained that William's sole interest in England, as earlier in Maine, was to obtain and hold his just inheritance against wrongful claimants. The legal and moral strength of William's case need not be discussed here. But we must allow him a case and an intention to operate within his ideas of law and justice. There is, therefore, much to be said for the view that William's original, and always basic, purpose was to slip into the shoes of his kinsman, Edward, and to take over his inheritance as a going concern. He would be prepared for some opposition, some disturbances. He would know that he would have to make some changes in order to secure his rule. But he would not expect to be disappointed in the value of the legacy. A crown and the traditional rights and revenues of the English king were as much as any heir could have desired. If Harold had not broken faith and opposed him, or if English resistance had then ceased, it is likely that William would have ruled in England, as in Maine, indeed as in all his dominions, essentially content with his inherited legal rights.

Although this attitude was distorted by events, it was never completely transformed. William developed no great liking for England or its inhabitants. He soon gave up his intention to learn the language. He only resided in the kingdom when it was necessary to see to its good order or defence. To the very end William grudged the drain on his time and energy that English complications caused. He was much happier fighting on his ducal frontiers. When he bequeathed Normandy to his eldest son, and England to his second son, William Rufus, he thereby broke up his empire – without a pang. We should not, therefore, imagine that the Conqueror had any premeditated or deliberate intention to make drastic changes in the English kingdom. He invaded to acquire a throne and its revenue, and with them dignity and glory.

William, however, did not become another Cnut. There was one prime difference between the situation in 1016 and in 1066. William and his army were more foreign than Cnut and his. Englishmen had become accustomed to Scandinavian rule; but in 1066 they did not recognize the Vikings in their new French dress. The English, as the Normans angrily or sorrowfully admitted, had no wish for a foreign king. By Christmas, when William was crowned, they were cowed or resigned. But when

William then light-heartedly returned to Normandy to celebrate his victory and display his spoils, and left the kingdom to
be ruled by his half-brother, Odo, bishop of Bayeux, and his
steward, William fitzOsbern, with their small garrison forces
confined to the south-eastern shires, the natives were not only
allowed to recover hope but also provoked into rebellion by
uncontrolled oppression.

Before Christmas 1067 William had to cut short his rejoicings
with his own people and return to his bridge-head in England.
His attempts to pacify the outraged population failed; he had to
begin to subdue the whole kingdom. By 1072 he had chastened
the south-west peninsular and East Anglia, conquered Mercia
and Northumbria, overawed the Cornish, Welsh and Scots,
and fought off Danish intervention. It was a war without
battles, a war of attrition. The English nobles conspired,
appealed for outside help, but acknowledged or found no real
leader. The succession of local uprisings were without true
military purpose. William was fighting the anarchy which
occurred whenever strong rule was removed, rather than a
national or patriotic resistance. Nevertheless the disturbances
were sufficient to strain his military resources and provoke
him and his commanders to savagery. The turn-over in his
army was considerable. Mercenary troops, driven hard, became
mutinous and would not re-engage. With the population hostile
or sullen, William's answer was to inspire terror, to harry and
destroy, and build castles to hold the devastated areas down.
The garrisons had to rob the villages.

The immediate effect, therefore, of William's coming was
widespread destruction. He and his troops were not the only
offenders. The rebels and their allies caused, perhaps, even
more. It was a convulsion typical of the period. Large areas of
agricultural land were wasted; most towns suffered some
damage; and famine and pestilence followed inevitably.

Atrocities were committed. The kingdom passed under military occupation and rule. Moreover, the English nobility was destroyed as a class and many of the native ecclesiastical leaders were deposed.

As William fought his way out of the chaos he began to proclaim symbolically the legitimacy of his rule; and then he and his followers did ecclesiastical penance for the sins committed in the war. In May 1068 the duchess Matilda crossed to England to be crowned queen by Archbishop Ealdred of York. She was already carrying the future King Henry I, and stayed in the kingdom until the boy was born. William was assuring the king-worthiness of at least one of his children. In 1070, while both archbishoprics were vacant, William was crowned by a papal legate. The taint of forceful entry was being washed away. Then, by papal authority and with the approval of the legate, the Norman bishops decreed the scale of penance for the victorious army. A careful distinction was drawn between the different categories of sinner (clerks, monks, laymen and, among the last, those who had the duty or command to follow the duke and those who were enrolled for gain) and between the various sins. Differently regarded were acts committed in the battle of Hastings, in the period between the battle and William's coronation, and after he had been crowned king. Further distinguished were the circumstances in which a man was slain, whether the killer was in search of food or of booty, whether the victim was in arms against the king or not. But adultery, fornication and rape, and the violation of churches, were allowed no special circumstances. Violators of churches were ordered to restore their thefts if they could, or, if not, give them to another church. In any case ecclesiastical property was to be neither sold nor purchased. Women who had been violated could not be indemnified. But later Archbishop Lanfranc ruled that women who had fled to nunneries and pretended to be nuns for fear of the French, could go out into the world again. The standard penance imposed in 1070 for killing was one year for each death, in aggravated circumstances three years or more. Most of these penances would have been commuted into the giving of alms or the building of a church. William built the monastery *de Bello* on the site of the great battle.

The church's attitude to the Conquest cannot be faulted. Even in a 'just' war sins had been committed and must be atoned for. Prayers would be said for the souls of the slain. There was no teaching, however, that reparations were due to the surviving victims of a public war. It was not a practical issue. General misery was too common. The English had suffered much from the heathen Vikings in the past. It would not appear that the destruction wrought in the relatively short period 1066–72 was on a larger scale. The resilient population, accustomed to hardship and practising a simple economy, could soon recover. There would be resentment for a time and then only the memory of catastrophe. Killing, rape, plunder, even in the usually well-governed English kingdom, were part of every-day life. The agricultural population could settle down again under its new lords. A Norman lord was not necessarily more oppressive than his English or Danish predecessor. There were no popular rebellions once turmoil had ceased. There was no patriotism in the modern sense in the villages, hamlets and towns.

Yet there was one special feature of Norman rule which could not easily be forgotten in what remained of the higher strata of English society. Even more shameful than the humiliations of the war was the disgrace that followed, especially the denial to the natives of high office. Under Cnut men had prophesied the return of a native king; and Edward had miraculously returned. But under the Norman kings men remembered and expounded that strange vision of a Green Tree, which, it was believed, Edward had experienced on his death-bed. According to the legend Edward was told by his heavenly visitors that God would cease punishing the English for their sins only 'when a green tree, if cut down in the middle of its trunk and the part cut off carried the space of three furlongs from the stock, shall be joined again to its trunk, by itself and without the hand of man, or any kind of stake, and begin once more to push leaves and bear fruit'.

The last commentator to regard it as a prophecy of perpetual doom for the conquered English was a Westminster monk, Osbert of Clare, writing in 1138, in the reign of Stephen, William's grandson. He wrote:

In good time they found out that the king's prophecy was true, when, after Harold's death in battle, rich England was conquered and submitted to Duke William, when [Archbishop] Stigand was deposed and condemned to life imprisonment . . . and lost irrevocably his position of honour. Also after the death of the glorious king [Edward] many thousands of Englishmen were slain. These things, because we are not writing a tragedy, . . . we will leave aside. But, before we resume, let us make perfectly clear what happened in the kingdom later, for the king, imbued with the spirit of God, foresaw, when he uttered this metaphor of impossibility, how difficult it would be in the future for the English to breathe again. Even today we no more see a king, nobleman, or bishop spring from that race than we see a felled tree rejoin its stock so that it may again push leaves and bear fruit.

Even during the reign of the last Norman king articulate Englishmen still believed that they were oppressed and being punished for their sins. Some of them were hailing as saints King Edward, who had ruled in peace like Solomon, and Earl Waltheof, by the Conqueror's command executed outside Winchester as a traitor. Only under Angevin rule did the

7. Motte and Bailey castle at Pleshey, Essex

8. Norman church at Melbourne, Derbyshire

distinction between English and Norman begin to lose significance.

The English remained depressed because within a decade of the
battle of Hastings the Anglo-Danish aristocracy, both ecclesiastical and lay, had been replaced by another which considered
itself French. This was the field in which J. H. Round worked;
and he had every reason to point to a revolution. All the men
who had been great in King Edward's reign and most of the
lesser nobility had been swept away. After the battle and
rebellions William, whether he had wanted it or not, had the
whole of England at his disposal. What is more, the native
nobility had to be replaced. William could not have administered the entire kingdom through officials; and his followers
would not have tolerated such greed. The new king reserved
to himself an enormous demesne, about a fifth of the arable
area, and out of the rest rewarded his kinsmen, vassals and
others who had a claim on his bounty.

William had made immediate provision in 1066 in England
south of the Thames for some of his key men. He himself held
London, Odo of Bayeux Dover and Kent, and William
fitzOsbern Winchester and the Isle of Wight. As English lords
were dispossessed in other areas, William and his closest
friends increased their holdings, and room was found for
others. No one was allowed to conquer for himself: the king
distributed the spoils, usually by allotting the estates of one or
more English 'traitors' to the donee; and so the overall pattern
which emerged, although it had novel features, was not
entirely unlike the old. There was again only a handful of really
large landholders. This select group included the royal family,
some Breton counts and the most favoured of William's
Norman vassals. But so great was the area to be distributed, and
so unusual the opportunity to be generous, that almost anyone

K

of the right breeding who could make a case was sure of a reward. The count of Boulogne and such other neighbouring counts as were William's vassals, and some Flemings and Bretons received their share. Many small Norman lords suddenly became rich. There were also the new king's personal servants, the lesser commanders in his army and some specialist soldiers for whom modest provision could be made. Not all the recipients thought that they had received their due reward, but few could have been completely disappointed. Then in turn the major beneficiaries rewarded their kinsmen, vassals and servants, and shared the king's bounty with their own followers.

The estates which the king distributed, and the barons subdivided, were usually old units, or multiples or parts of them. In geographical appearance they were loosely grouped, but normally round some centre, where there was a closer concentration. With the larger estates, sometimes rather haphazardly assembled, there could be several foci and wider spacing. In these features there was no change. William, however, broke the old pattern of earldoms. Only one Edwardian earldom was spared, and this owing to unusual circumstances. Waltheof, earl of Huntingdon, the son of Earl Siward of Northumbria, married William's niece and added Northumberland in 1072. After his execution in 1076 their daughter, Matilda, carried the joint honour to her two husbands in turn, and it passed, almost alternatively, to the descendants of each. The great Anglo-Danish provincial earldoms (really duchies) were, however, discontinued.

In Edward's reign Ralf had held a marcher earldom against the Welsh; and Harold's Wessex and Tostig's Northumbria could be regarded as dukedoms which protected the south and north against attack. William developed the system much further by ringing England, like Normandy, with border

counties. Northumberland, Richmond, Chester, Shrewsbury
Hereford, Cornwall and Kent were each entrusted to a faithful
vassal, who was made the sole or most important secular land-
holder in his county and given the duty of defending the
frontier. It was an essential feature only of the conquest
period, and, with the growth of security, some of the structure
was allowed to collapse. No successor was appointed to Roger
of Hereford in 1075 or Odo of Kent in 1082. Later creations –
Surrey and Warwick (William II), Buckingham, Leicester
and Gloucester (Henry I), Derby, Hertford, Pembroke,
Worcester, York, Arundel, Cambridge, Lincoln, Essex and
Norfolk (Stephen), and Devon, Somerset, Oxford and Salisbury (Matilda) – rarely had a true strategic purpose. The title of
earl was conferred as a reward and honour.

The redistribution of the lands of England among the
French was both a grant of revenue and a military occupation.
The new landholders acquired all the rents and services which
their predecessors had enjoyed. In an economic context the
change of lords made little difference to the agricultural pro-
ducers, the farmers and their labourers, the small-holders and
the stock breeders. There were many rough actions and mis-
understandings; there may occasionally have been new men
with new ideas. Sometimes there was a determined effort to
restock under-exploited estates. There may have been a general
movement to require full economic rents. But the incoming
lords, certainly the major barons, were mostly absentees. The
men who enjoyed William's greatest trust, and received the
largest estates in England, he used as his captains in the Norman
wars. These may have pressed heavily on their stewards,
reeves and other agents to increase the revenues from their
estates; but they had no revolutionary means of exploitation.

More noticeable in the countryside was the military aspect
of lordship. The English nobles had kept retainers, who rode

and on occasion fought beside them. Often these vassals held or were granted land. But English halls were defended only by a ditch and palisade or hedge. The lords had no true military strongholds. The Conquest made a great change. William built castles in the more important towns to hold royal garrisons and enable his armies to move in stages throughout the kingdom. His vassals built private castles to protect their estates. Under Stephen, the last of the Norman kings, a new wave of castle-building spread through the country, a result of the civil wars. These baronial castles were mostly simple constructions of earth and timber and were often allowed to decay in peaceful times. But a new feature, the basin-like mound of the motte, had been added to the English landscape.

The replacement of an Anglo-Danish by a French aristo-cracy was bound to affect the social customs in the kingdom. It is true that the Norman, Breton, Flemish and other French barons were, in education, interests and outlook, not unlike the thegns and earls whom they replaced. A few Normans and Bretons had settled in England during Edward's reign; Earl Harold had probably not felt a complete stranger in William's army when he joined the duke for the Breton campaign of 1064. There were many minor differences in the social conven-tions, and there was the barrier of language; but there was no greater cleavage in culture – indeed probably less – than, say, between English and Norman landlords to-day. We may be sure that the Normans who were granted estates in England by William could have assumed the role of their predecessors without much adjustment had they so wished. Even the lan-guage barrier could have been short-lived. The Normans were an adaptable people; their ancestors had learned French; and the generation which would be born in the English king-dom could be encouraged to be bi-lingual.

Yet French customs did not yield as quickly as Scandinavian

in the past. There was the absence of English social equals. The English language was spoken by inferiors and sounded barbarous to the French. English personal names especially were considered ridiculous and uncouth. Conversely the conquered were soon tempted to imitate the new aristocracy. English parents began to give their children Norman names. All with social pretensions who came in contact with the foreigners aspired to speak French. On most large estates there remained a number of Englishmen in the class between the newcomers and the farmers, 'squires' with modest estates. These were to be the intermediaries, bi-lingual, but with English as the cradle tongue, and often aspiring to marry into the middle or lower strata of Norman society. There were also the less privileged Normans, priests and servants, who were glad to marry English women. In mercantile society there was little prejudice on either side. But if such contacts eased the recovery of English culture they also more effectively helped the spread of French. To behave like the French had become the mark of gentility.

Throughout the Norman period, therefore, the French formed a fairly exclusive circle. It is possible that Henry I and his nephew, Stephen, could understand a little English; but they did not speak it: they had no need to. When William II took over the duchy of Normandy, when Henry I conquered it, when Stephen of Blois, count of Mortain and Boulogne, became king, when Matilda, countess of Anjou, invaded, there were new influxes of foreigners. The oldest established colonists were settling down, racial antagonism was dying fast, but there was enough renewal of French influence at the top to keep the new culture alive.

The Norman settlers brought their laws and customs with them and had no wish for change. All who received a grant of land took it as a fief held on conditions, and acknowledged that

K 2

they were the vassals of the donor. It does not seem that the early grants were normally made in writing, by charter, or that the conditions of tenure were explicitly rehearsed. We may assume that the grantor expected the grantee to perform all the services for which the land was traditionally liable and also the duties of a vassal as generally understood at the time. The vassal would owe his lord fealty and loyalty, service in his court, escort and defence duties, and would fight under his lord's flag on military campaign. The lord and his vassals formed a family: each owed the other comfort and protection. The vassal was expected to aid his lord in every way, and the lord was required to watch over his vassal's interests, and make provision for his widow or orphaned children. The act of homage and the oath of fealty created a social bond.

This great series of enfeoffments, made within a short period, is often regarded as the introduction of feudalism into England. It should rather be regarded as a unique event which had unique results. There was in Europe in the eleventh century great variety in social and legal customs: there were some obvious national distinctions, many regional cultures and the individual peculiarities of each lordship. Yet there were common features, which are usually described as feudal: vassalage, military groupings and ideals, and the fragmentation of authority. Even if we hold to the basic meaning of feudal – pertaining to a fief – we shall still not rule the Old-English kingdom out of this system, for varieties of the fief were certainly present in England. It is better, therefore, to regard the tenurial revolution which occurred after the Conquest as the creator of a new type of feudalism, one different as much from the Norman as from the Old-English. It was one made in England in special circumstances.

Anglo-Norman feudalism differed from both English and Norman in its conceptual uniformity and logical structure.

Although it had probably been accepted that all land belonged ultimately to the king of the English, and Norman dukes may have felt that all Normandy ultimately belonged to them, only after the Conquest was it publicly demonstrated that the whole of the kingdom was in the king's gift. Moreover, all the major estates, except royal demesne and a few churches, mostly abbeys, were granted, within the space of a decade, as fiefs, and those that escaped the first forfeiture and re-grant received the same treatment later. Thus William divided England into great fiefs or 'honours'. The laymen to whom he granted them were his vassals or, as they came to be called in England, his barons. These men, when they rewarded their own vassals, likewise granted them fiefs. In practice within a relatively short time, certainly by the time of Domesday Book, there had arisen every tenurial complexity which can be imagined: barons holding fiefs of each other, and of their own or of another's vassal; mesne-tenants holding fiefs of several lords and of each other. Only if we disregard all these complications can we talk of a feudal pyramid, with the king at its apex. Yet the Domesday commissioners could solve every tenurial tangle by asking, 'From whom do you hold the land?' They were recording links in a chain which ultimately, they knew, would reach the king. And each link was bonded to the next by homage and fealty.

Once the main enfeoffments had been made, the law of each honour began to form. Men, sometimes bred to different customs, were entering into new relationships in strange conditions. There were enough common assumptions for them to rub along, especially during the period of danger, when lords and their vassals were engaged in a joint enterprise and there was no time for trivial legal disputes. As time passed, however, and all the problems emerged which had to be settled by law, the law had to be declared; and through judgements made by the suitors in the honorial courts the law of the honour was formed. There were innumerable matters which had to be decided: the exact services due from a vassal to his lord, on what terms could a fief or part of it be alienated, who had the wardship of a vassal's children under age, when could a lord claim an aid or relief, and so on. The influence of the king's court and the interlocking of the honours hindered extreme individuality of custom in the several baronies; but diversity there was. It was also a changing body of custom. It is a mistake to regard medieval customs as static: unwritten law could easily be altered. And it seems that after the first period of stability, reached in the reign of Henry I, the novel conditions under Stephen required a revision of the law in most honours. English feudal custom was still developing when, with the growth of the competence and activity of the royal court under the Angevins, it was checked and began to lose its vitality.

One of the great effects of the Conquest, therefore, was the creation of a new body of law in the kingdom. As it was formed by the French, and at first affected few who were not French, it owed little directly to the English past, although it should not be regarded as something completely alien. A Harold or a Leofric could have quickly adjusted himself to the new society and would not necessarily have found its rules uncongenial. It owed much to Norman and French custom; but it was made in England to meet English conditions. A branch of it, the law of the king's court, became eventually the common law of the land. Yet the king's justices often declared the law when on eyre in the shire court, where Old-English law ran; and when we trace the later history of English law it is difficult to be sure what contribution, either in substance or in procedure, was made by the Normans. We can point to minor features, such as the *duellum* (ordeal by combat, and pleading in French. But it would be rash to hold that important principles of twelfth- and thirteenth-century English law, such as the indefeasibility of private rights, the importance of possession, the necessity for a just judgement of a court before execution of sentence and judgement by peers, were more Norman than English in origin. Nor can some vital procedural habits, such as the original writ or trial by jury, be assigned an exclusive Norman provenance. In any case they were not the inventions of the honorial courts.

When we pass from law to social attitudes we enter an even less tangible world. One military society, with basically northern traditions, had been replaced by another which had imitated its customs from France. There were differences between the two, and, although all attempts to portray them tend to become caricatures, we can do no more than generalize. The Old-English nobility had been nurtured more comfortably. There was a tradition of literacy among them and, in the eleventh century, a fondness for luxury. Men wore their hair long and cultivated social graces. The Bayeux Tapestry depicts their elegance. The Normans, although they took pride in their dress and food, were rougher, less cultured, less sophisticated. At first they considered their crudity a virtue and mocked at the English nobles whom they thought as beautiful as girls. But with English wealth they soon aped some English fashions, and by William II's reign moralists were denouncing their effeminacy. The two races had a different attitude towards women. In Anglo-Saxon society women were held in typical northern respect. They held land and could leave it by will. Norman society was more masculine; manners were those of the camp and castle. William I showed small interest in women; William Rufus was a homosexual; and Henry I, although a lecher, was said to take no pleasure in his mistresses. A few ladies made their mark in this rough world, but only by displaying masculine virtues.

Within half a century of the Conquest, however, some of

these attitudes were disappearing among the Normans. It was not unusual for the grandsons, and especially the grand-daughters, of the Domesday baronage to receive some education. During the course of the twelfth century women began to cultivate their own interests and to have influence over men. We notice the first faint effects of courtly love and of the French romance. Society manners would not have developed in quite the same way if the aristocracy had remained English or if the newcomers had adopted the vernacular speech. But the Norman contribution was to provide the vehicle, the language, for the new ideas rather than the ideas themselves. It is difficult to point to any strand in gentility which was purely Norman. The standards were French, and remained so under the Angevins.

Within and above the feudal society was the king. William I had no direct experience of strong monarchy. He was familiar with some aspects of royalty through his close contact with his weak Capetian overlord; and he was aware that there were stronger kings in Germany and England. With such a background he must have viewed the rights of an English king as something to grasp and retain, not as something in obvious need of reform. Nevertheless, between 1066 and 1154 the royal administration changed considerably in detail. Changes would have occurred without the Norman conquest. Royal government had made amazing strides in England between 899 and 1066 and there is no reason to suppose that stagnation would have set in with the accession of Harold. Moreover, few of the innovations can be assigned a purely Norman origin or attributed to characteristic Norman genius. They were mostly demanded by alterations in the circumstances. Norman achievement was to re-establish traditional English monarchy, modify it to suit the new conditions and develop it prag-matically as need arose.

If we look at the period as a whole it seems that the Conqueror, faced with the collapse of his inheritance, improvised at every turn to keep the traditional administration going; William Rufus gave stability to the makeshift organization; Henry I and his ministers brought fresh eyes to bear on many aspects of royal government, and, by tidying up, not only produced greater efficiency in the old system but also gave it new lines of advance; and, finally, in the war of succession after Henry's death this fine administrative achievement was sadly disturbed although not broken. The first two kings had habits of government but no constructive ideas. They contributed little to the monarchy except power. Henry I was intelligent and creative. He did not, however, contribute Norman solutions to English problems. On the contrary, when he conquered Normandy from his brother he introduced English practices into the duchy. By 1135 it may well have appeared to the Normans that they had been conquered by England. The weaker and poorer partner had been taken over by the revitalized kingdom.

The most obvious effect of the Norman conquest was that the king became a frequent absentee. English kings, except Cnut, had hitherto always resided in the kingdom. William and his successors, when they were also duke of Normandy and count of Maine, had to make provision for the government of England to continue in their absence. The natural arrangement would have been for a member of the royal family, assisted by a baronial council, to act as regent. William I made such a provision for Normandy and Henry I occasionally for England. But as the Conqueror had no kinsman to whom he wanted to entrust England, and William II was unmarried, the important tradition was created that the king could be represented by one of his servants, normally a bishop. Henry I gave this arrangement institutional form. About 1109, soon after he had dispossessed his brother of Normandy, he appointed standing deputies, with the title of justiciar, in both England and Normandy, and for each he created a fixed local court, which became known as the English or Norman exchequer. Roger le Poer, a chaplain who had been trained in Henry's household, and had risen to be royal chancellor and then bishop of Salisbury, was the first holder of the office in England. His opposite number in Normandy was John, bishop of Lisieux. Both these men, through sons or nephews, founded clerical dynasties which were to give the monarchy devoted service and facilitate the continuity of the administration into the Angevin period.

Until this decisive step was taken, the royal court changed little except in a superficial way. There was a change in nomenclature. The thegns, stallers, Housecarles and clerks at court were replaced, some quickly, some gradually, by men performing similar functions, but increasingly French by birth and soon bearing the titles of the Capetian court: stewards, butlers, chamberlains, marshals, constables and chaplains. Also two new officials appear: the chaplain in charge of the writing office is named chancellor and the clerk in charge of the royal hoard, treasurer. But there was continuity for a time in the administrative branches of the household. William took over all the apparatus he could: the royal clerks with their skills, the writ-charter, the royal seal, the financial system and coinage. The language of the writs was soon changed from English to Latin, but not, we notice, into French. Like Edward and all contemporary princes, William and his successors were always accompanied by their household and trusted counsellors. At the great church festivals they, like Edward, held more solemn courts, when they were crowned anew, sat enthroned in majesty to impress the visitors, feasted their vassals and sometimes took wider counsel. It is impossible to say in what particulars the Conqueror's courts and councils differed from

Edward's. No contemporary noted a change except in the persons attending. Henry I, more parsimonious than his brother and less primitive than his father, probably reduced a little the more ostentatious aspects of royalty. But, as we shall see, he had his own contributions to make.

The other most obvious effect of the Conquest was the re-endowment of the monarchy. Owing to the demands made on royal generosity and the need to reward servants, royal demesne tended to diminish. Kings became entitled to services, which could not always be enforced, instead of revenue with which services could be hired. Hereditary monarchies were usually in the end starved out. Changes of dynasty enriched the monarchy, for the new king added his private estates to the royal demesne, although, if the usurper was weak, he had many debts to repay, much loyalty to buy. In 1066 Harold restored the royal demesne by adding Wessex. William through confiscation did even better. Then, under his two sons, the process was reversed until Stephen contributed his own and his wife's English estates. Stephen, however, was by nature and necessity generous.

William I also increased the royal demesne by creating the 'royal forest'. He reserved large areas of England, irrespective of tenure and the mode of cultivation, for his hunting. His sons arbitrarily added to these preserves, but at the cost of un-popularity. Henry I had to agree at his coronation to give up Rufus's afforestations, and Stephen was faced with episcopal and baronial demands for a reduction. The forest, as well as providing sport, was a source of revenue. The venison and boars were for the table; the royal monopoly of timber was of some value; and there were the fines and penalties for breaches of the special forest law.

There is no evidence that any of the Norman kings radically reformed the administration of the royal demesne. Estates in the several counties were 'farmed' by royal servants, principally the sheriffs, and the agreed rents, together with casual profits, but less authorized disbursements, were paid into the king's chamber or the royal treasury at Winchester. The Norman kings seem to have pressed harder in other directions. Geld, the tax levied on estates according to their hidage, was re-instituted by the Conqueror and imposed annually. Feudal rights were fully exploited: the kings demanded a heavy, sometimes extortionate, relief when an heir succeeded to an honour, insisted on the right of wardship and marriage when the children of a deceased baron were under age, and, on occasion, requested an aid from their vassals. Some of these feudal rights had English parallels, some were new. The kings also made men pay for every favour and even more heavily to avoid its loss; but they were hardly innovating here. Henry I had to promise at his coronation to abate some of the more unpopular fiscal measures of his brother. He did not honour his promise in full. Stephen, less secure, had to make more effective concessions.

The Conqueror's passionate interest in his royal rights has as its monument the two volumes of Domesday Book. At Christmas 1085 William ordered a survey of his kingdom to be made; and it was substantially completed before the end of the following year. The inquest was carried out by royal commissioners who required the landholders and their estate agents to provide information which was then checked in the local courts. The survey records, shire by shire, the estates of the king and his tenants-in-chief. It was a record of present tenures and ancient duties. Among the obligations were the pecuniary value of the estate (its rentable value) and the hidage (its rateable value). The economic statistics which were collected – area under cultivation, manpower and equipment (the figures for stock were collected but omitted from the final summary) and profitable rights – provided the means by which the values could be checked or reconsidered. Despite its inaccuracies, Domesday Book could provide the answers to many questions of vital interest both to the king and his barons; and it could have been of use to a fiscal or military reformer, for geld and military service were based on the hidage. The Conqueror, however, did not live to profit by it, and it is doubtful whether his successors showed much interest in its potentialities. They concentrated on exploiting their traditional rights rather than on general reform.

The broad pattern of royal financial administration remained unchanged from the Old-English period. It was vital that there should be proper audit at all levels; and the one clear innovation in the Norman period was Henry I's decision that the justiciars should audit the accounts of some of the royal financial agents in their exchequer court. Records of some aspects of the audit, especially of outstanding debts and judicial decisions on fiscal matters, were kept; and the English Pipe Rolls, of which one example survives from the reign of Henry I, form one of the earliest and longest-running series of royal records.

The existence of these rolls and the *mystique* of the exchequer auditing procedure have, however, led to a common misunderstanding of Norman and Angevin royal finance and have often created the impression that it was more sophisticated than it really was. In fact, by 1135 no substantial advance had been made on Anglo-Saxon practice. All royal moneys were the king's and for and at his pleasure. His chamber, in which he kept his spending money, remained, therefore, at the centre of the system. For the king the importance of the English and Norman exchequers in this capacity was simply that they squeezed every penny out of his debtors. For us they are proof that Henry I and his advisers could improve the administrative machinery by introducing the best techniques available at the time.

As the Norman kings were wealthy they were less dependent than many of their contemporaries on the physical services of their vassals. In England the Conqueror was at first short of troops; and in the years of turmoil every soldier who could be raised was required for indefinite periods of service. Although William and his principal captains usually commanded mercenary armies, the new earls and barons were obliged to call out not only their own vassals but also those Englishmen who owed the king military service. William had Englishmen in his army as early as 1067 and later they fought in France and Maine. Barons were encouraged to build castles and recruit soldiers to garrison them. For at least a decade the Normans organized themselves for war. Once order had been re-established, however, both the king and his barons began to lose interest in these special arrangements. The barons counted the cost. The king still needed the services of his barons, but more discriminately. He kept his most important English barons and some of their forces with him on the Continent; in England he appointed bishops as his deputy military commanders and reduced the army to little above minimum garrison strength. In 1085, when a Danish invasion threatened, he had to bring a large mercenary force to England.

We may be confident that the reciprocal obligations of the king and his tenants-in-chief were not minutely defined either at the time of grant or later: the subsequent history of their relations gives ample proof of uncertainty, and some matters which came into dispute were not settled before Magna Carta in 1215. A few contentious matters, especially military, were not determined even then. J. H. Round, however (and he was followed by most of his successors), believed that one aspect of military tenure, the strength of the contingents owed by the king's vassals, was fixed almost immediately. At some point, according to Round, each of the tenants-in-chief was awarded by the Conqueror the service of an arbitrary quota of knights. But a recent investigation of the evidence by Mr H. G. Richardson and Professor G. O. Sayles goes far to re-affirm the general rule. In their view definition of military service was achieved gradually through disputes, royal acts of benevolence or of punishment, and the hardening of custom; the first general determination of the *servitia debita* took place under Henry II; and this settlement was soon modified again. Moreover, and here the evidence is strong, the general tendency was towards a reduction of the duty. It is doubtful whether any earl, baron, bishop or abbot owed as much military service in 1166 as he would have been liable for, from the same lands, under Edward the Confessor.

William and his sons relaxed their inherited claim to the military service of their vassals not through weakness but because the system was anachronistic. Their great achievement was to transform it into a source of revenue. Increasingly they dispensed with the unsatisfactory duty-contingents, accepted a fine or scutage in lieu and used the money to hire the professional troops they required. So their vassals, with small opportunity for fighting either among themselves or in the royal wars on the Continent, began to lose their military appearance. Even though the disputed succession after Henry I's death reanimated military interests, most English barons showed little belligerency. Stephen relied much on Flemish mercenaries; and both the loyal and the rebel barons were concerned far more with the defence of their own estates during the relaxation of government than with aggression. They even made treaties among themselves in order to limit private war. The few exceptions, such as Geoffrey de Mandeville, were considered malefactors by both sides.

The Conquest, far from developing the military aspect of society, clearly reduced it. The kingdom was defended by the king fighting with largely professional armies in and around Normandy. A few important military units were allowed to develop in the English marches, and some of these retained their vitality; but, after the first years, nothing was done to encourage the military significance of the honours. At Salisbury in 1086 William took an oath of fealty from important rear-vassals as well as from his tenants-in-chief. Private castles came increasingly under royal control and disapproval. English society under Henry I was certainly less organized for war than it had been under Edward. No longer were there earls, like Harold and Tostig, with large private armies of mercenaries and vassals. No more did men from the shires expect to be summoned to the royal army. The civil war in Stephen's reign was nothing compared to the fighting under Æthelred or in the quinquennium after 1065. After the Conquest rich malcontents could hire troops and rebel; but the king was always richer. Anglo-Norman feudalism was feudalism tamed by royal power.

The dominance which the Norman kings exerted over their vassals can also be seen in the sphere of justice; and the rapid decay of military feudalism was itself partly due to royal insistence on the observance of the law and the determination of disputes by legal trial. One immediate effect of the Conquest was an increase in disorder, crime and disputes over land. William used every available method to keep the courts working. He guaranteed to each race its own law, confirmed to every man his just rights and made provision for a conflict of laws. The king and his barons held courts for their own vassals; but it was essential that the territorial courts – shire, hundred and 'manorial' – should continue to function, for it was in these that English law ran. By 1072 the ranks of the shire thegns, the men who knew the law and the history of estates, was thinned, and William improvised to keep the local courts running: meetings of groups of shires or hundreds were convoked, judges appointed to oversee several shires, judges dispatched from the royal court to hear an important case in the locality, local justiciars appointed to help the sheriff in judicial work. In time barons and knights of French descent learned their duties as suitors and judges in the shire court. Too much attention can be given to the, almost invisible, honorial courts: their jurisdiction was largely confined to domestic disputes. The shire and hundred courts remained the basic tribunals.

Once the Norman kings had embarked on the policy of maintaining the old local courts and keeping the honorial courts in check, they had to develop the judicial functions of their own *curia*. It had to be more than the court for the king's own vassals; it had to oversee and supplement the local courts, to take ultimate responsibility for the dispensation of justice throughout the kingdom. In this policy Norman aims and Old-English practice came together, and interesting developments took place, especially under Henry I.

Henry not only took new steps to reanimate the local courts, and increased the judicial activities of his own, but also brought the two into powerful conjunction. On his side he created the justiciar and his exchequer court and as well sent judges on general eyre through the kingdom. These men visited the county courts, where the hundreds were represented, scrutinized their conduct, heard criminal cases reserved to the king (the pleas of the crown), investigated all categories of royal rights and heard important land cases, or common pleas as they came to be called. Most cases were still heard in the local courts, whether territorial or seigneurial; but important cases, and especially those in which the king had an interest, could be heard before the king's justices in eyre, before the justiciar at the exchequer or by the king himself. It was a flexible, simple system. There was one royal court, dividing and re-forming according to convenience, and capable of reaching out into almost every locality. The same royal justices sat with the king or the justiciar and went on eyre. They were not professionals, but omni-competent royal servants; yet most future juridical developments were already present in germ. Cases were being originated by obtaining a royal writ; juries of presentment and trial juries were being sworn. Juries are often regarded as a Norman innovation imitated from Frankish practice. It is a very dark subject. But we should notice that English juries are most in evidence when the ancient courts of shire and hundred meet royal judges. Although the king and his justices may have moulded the pattern, the sworn evidence of local communities seems to have been an Old-English as well as a Frankish custom.

William I and his sons exploited English kingship to the best of their ability. Although some historians have regarded it as a new monarchy, it is doubtful whether the Normans contributed any completely new strand. Lordship was nothing new. No new struggle for power, with the king allying with the English against his barons, came suddenly into existence. The interests of the king and his barons were not basically opposed: normally they shared a class, even a family, interest. It is true that individual barons resented the king's use of his power, and on the death of each king there was a general reaction against strong rule. Such outbursts were not new in English history. It is also true that the English looked to the king against local oppression and in moments of crisis would support him against aristocratic rebellion; but that too had been a feature of the past. This is not to say that there was no change. With both the monarchy and the nobility strengthened there was more chance of conflict; and there began that running debate between the king and his barons over rights and duties which led to a constitution. The charter extorted by the barons and church from Henry I at his coronation, promising relief from the bad customs introduced by his brother, even if ineffective at the time, proved to be an important precedent. However traditional the powers wielded by the Norman kings may have been, they were given new impetus, a special development, a Norman interpretation. But no Norman king based a claim on the ducal past. All men looked to the laws of King Edward. To Henry I, like Edward, men attributed thaumaturgical powers: Henry could touch for the King's Evil. And in Stephen's reign the first attempt was made, supported by the king, to get Edward canonized. Under Henry, William, monk of Malmesbury, wrote in separate books of the deeds of the kings and prelates of England. Under Stephen, Geoffrey of Monmouth wrote his *History of the Britons*. English law and practice was collected and expounded. The parvenu Normans were appropriating Old-English history.

In no sphere is our main theme illustrated more pointedly than in the ecclesiastical. The church, by its nature resistant to revolution, is by its character most susceptible to reform. All churches are almost constantly criticized by some of their members for falling short of an ideal; unfamiliar ecclesiastical customs are usually regarded unfavourably by aliens; and an institution without hereditary succession and in which deposition from office is possible can be given a new appearance in a relatively short time.

After the Conquest the English church, with a long, unbroken history and deep-seated insular customs, rich, artistic, unique in its vernacular culture, was viewed with largely hostile eyes by men educated in another tradition. As a result there was considerable change. But again it was a complex process. As there were already in the English church several foreign bishops and abbots besides Englishmen anxious for reform, and the Norman church itself was ruled to an even greater degree by foreigners, there could be no simple confrontation of English and Norman ideals. Moreover, most of the more important developments in the English church after 1066 were not of Norman inspiration. The new factors, such as the growth of papal monarchy and the rising standards in education, would have affected England whatever the political events might have been.

The immediate Norman attitude towards the church they found was extremely mixed. Although they were awed by its splendour, they despised its customs and culture, and also coveted its wealth. They disliked its archaic Roman liturgy, its buildings in an out-moded style and its incomprehensible learning. Moreover, William had clerical claimants on his generosity and himself wanted bishops whom he could trust absolutely, who could serve as his vice-regents in the kingdom. The answer was reform, for this could cover all motives. In 1070 William, through papal connivance, secured the legal deposition of those bishops whom he wished to remove, and the newcomers examined the fitness of the abbots. The break with the past, however, came more slowly than is often realized. English abbots of unimportant houses persisted for some time. Even in 1087 there were still on the episcopal bench one of Edward's English bishops and two men who had been his clerks. But as William and his sons steadfastly refused to promote Englishmen to high ecclesiastical office, the superstructure became completely foreign, although not exclusively Norman. At the same time, as in the secular sphere, the much larger infra-structure remained almost untouched. The monastic communities were only gradually, and never entirely, normanized. There was almost no interference with the village priests.

At first the natives and denizens reciprocated Norman contempt. Goscelin of St Bertin, a Flemish monk who had made his home in England, wrote, shortly after 1080, of the newcomers:

> Those who forbid scholarship through fear of pride . . . would do far better to learn through education how to preserve humility . . . and eradicate the barbarous pride and bragging of the undisciplined. We shall soon see the unlearned deriding and despising the learned and counting illiteracy secular wisdom or holiness of life. No wonder . . . ignorant men take pride in the cult of humility.

Edward, archdeacon of London, who became a monk of Christ Church, Canterbury, under Lanfranc, tried to run away again, tired of being corrected by men inferior to himself in learning. It must be clearly appreciated that the prelates appointed by the Norman kings – the bishops usually royal chaplains rewarded for their services – were not as a whole in a different class, as regards spirituality or scholarship, from those promoted by their English predecessors.

The death of the archbishop of York in 1069 and the deposition of the archbishop of Canterbury in 1070, together with the other displacements, forced the newcomers to review and settle the organization of the church. William and Archbishop Lanfranc of Canterbury, sharing the ideal of a sharp hierarchical structure, insisted that Canterbury had the primacy not only over England but over all the British Isles, defined the two English provinces, again in a way unfavourable to York, and reaffirmed the subjection of the bishops to their metropolitan. Bishops were ordered to remove their see, if unsatisfactorily placed, to a city, and to appoint proper ecclesiastical officials. The dioceses were divided into archdeaconries and these in course of time into rural deaneries. This structural redefinition, since it respected both ancient history and ancient geography, was to last little changed for centuries. Lanfranc's primacy could not be maintained in all its amplitude and Henry I created a new diocese in each province, Ely and Carlisle. But the experimental revisions of the diocesan boundaries carried out in the late Old-English period were ignored and never tried again.

Lanfranc held a few legislative councils at the beginning of his rule, in which some common abuses were condemned and the bishops were ordered to reform their dioceses. Archbishop Anselm took up the task again in Henry I's reign, and there was much conciliar activity under Stephen. But the essential feature of Anglo-Norman ecclesiastical government was the responsibility of the bishops, under metropolitan guidance, for the government of the church. There was nothing novel in this or in the spiritual charge. Simony (the selling of spiritual offices and services) was no special problem in England; the marriage and sexual immorality of the clergy was a problem everywhere. The drive against the latter sin was set in motion again by enacting the moderate rules of the Norman church against offenders. But, as everything depended on the zeal of the diocesan bishop, the effect was unequal. The most zealous persecutor of the married clergy seems to have been the Englishman, St Wulfstan of Worcester.

More successful than the moral reform was the reorganization of episcopal administration and justice. The new bishops found that in England they lacked some of the rights which their brethren enjoyed in Normandy. These were granted to them by William. They were to have a monopoly of the ordeals and unfettered spiritual jurisdiction in their dioceses. They quickly appointed their own justiciars and archdeacons and began to withdraw cases, and their profits, from the shire and hundred courts into their own synods and tribunals. No encouragement was given to monastic claims to exemption from episcopal jurisdiction: Lanfranc dealt harshly with St Augustine's, Canterbury. Nor did most Norman bishops care for the monastic communities which in some dioceses served the cathedral church. But an initial attempt to suppress them was frustrated by English indignation to which Lanfranc and then the pope rallied. Where there were cathedral chapters formed of clerks or canons the bishops began to refashion them on Norman lines.

The new bishops almost immediately began the rebuilding of their cathedral church. They had little initial respect for the English past, pulled down the ancient edifices with their holy associations, and, wealthy, ambitious, determined to impress, began noble structures which, when they have survived, still impress to-day. The remains of English saints, buried in the churches, were often treated roughly. But the disinterments and the question of the translation of the relics, aroused curiosity, for the new masters quite understandably refused to treat as saints men who had no legend. The result was much historical research in the communities and the production of a new corpus of hagiographical writings in Latin, which not only preserved the history of the English church but also helped towards devotional continuity.

Many of the monasteries suffered severely at first. They were centres of vernacular culture and conservative in temper. Norman austerity and discipline aroused no initial enthusiasm. But they soon became centres of reconciliation, where English and Norman could live together, pursuing a common ideal. Eadmer and Osbern, both Englishmen, gave fame to Christ Church, Canterbury; the Anglo-Fleming Goscelin eventually found honour at St Augustine's. In some houses, like Worcester and Peterborough, English traditions remained strong. The Normans were not speculative or outstandingly artistic. There was no more interest in England in theology, canon law or dialectics after 1066 than before, possibly less. The Burgundian Anselm, the greatest light of the age, found small welcome in England. But the island could hardly remain entirely untouched by the new ferment of ideas in the western

L

church; and in Henry I's reign there was a reflorescence of art and literature in the monasteries. The tightening of discipline and the modifications in the Rule had served to create balanced, purposeful communities. In the same period some of the new religious orders began to settle in the kingdom, their primitive austerity and sense of vocation needling those Benedictine houses which had mellowed.

The Conquest gave the English church a new look. Externally there was the rebuilding, internally the thorough administrative reorganization and the replacement of the vernacular culture by one more Latin and French in tone. As in secular society, the cleavage between the higher and the lower ranks had been widened. Yet it would be a mistake to think that there was a novel cleavage between the church and the laity. It is true that the reanimated ecclesiastical government gave the church a more distinct appearance and that the purpose of the reformers was to insist on the difference between the two orders; but in social attitudes the Normans were as conservative as the English. The Conqueror, accustomed to ruling the Norman church, exercised the ecclesiastical rights of an English king without hesitation, and may well have extended them. He appointed to bishoprics and royal abbeys; he demanded temporal services from his ecclesiastical vassals; he presided over ecclesiastical councils or licensed their actions. More novel, perhaps, he restricted the church's power to exercise justice over his barons and servants, and closely controlled its intercourse with Rome. In the face of papal schism he ruled that no pope could be recognized in England without royal approval, and, noting the growth of papal interference in domestic affairs, he insisted that all correspondence with Rome should pass through his hands and no papal legate should enter the kingdom without his permission. The English church remained a national church, with the king its effective head.

William rebuffed all novel claims that emanated from the reformed papacy. He would not hold England as a papal fief, he would not allow his archbishops to be ordered about by the pope. Indeed, when Gregory VII lost Rome, the English church seems to have acknowledged no outside superior, a situation which William Rufus was pleased to prolong.

As the Conqueror was a religious prince who encouraged the church to perform its moral and pastoral duties, and his bishops were accustomed to secular direction, a stable organization was created which could hardly be rocked either from within by the careless and impious rule of his successor or from without by the radical ideas of 'Gregorian' reformers. Rufus, by exploiting the wealth of the church in many ingenious ways, tried its patience sorely; but it bore his exactions with fortitude. Henry I, a reformer of his father's type, had, however, to solve a problem which had already disturbed most of Christendom.

The Conqueror's practice, usual at the time, and possibly not unknown in England, was to invest prelates with their office by conferring the spiritual symbols. Some extreme ecclesiastical reformers on the Continent, were, however, demanding the complete independence of the church from secular control, and even the more moderate were seeking the abolition of lay investiture, which for them symbolized the evil. England remained sheltered from the debate and strife, partly because of ingrained conservatism, partly because of papal forbearance; and by the time the issue was forced on Henry I by Archbishop Anselm on his return from exile, some of the heat had already gone out of the controversy. Henry manoeuvred adroitly, and in the end suggested a compromise which accorded with the more moderate ideas of the time. He would abandon investiture by ring and staff, but would retain the taking of homage and fealty from the prelate-elect. It was also tacitly accepted that he would continue to enjoy his ecclesiastical patronage.

A new power was arising in Christendom to which even English kings and bishops had to give heed. But the development of ecclesiastical institutions and pretensions within the kingdom and the growth of papal interference, both noticeable in Stephen's reign, were hardly in any sense a direct result of the Norman conquest. Two opposing tendencies have to be borne in mind: the union of England and Normandy facilitated the entry of new ideas for which the Normans themselves were not responsible, which, indeed, they often disliked; but the impact of these was delayed by strong Norman kingship, behind which shield most prelates preferred to shelter.

It can hardly be denied that the effects of the Norman conquest were wide and lasting. Had the kingdom remained Anglo-Danish, within a Scandinavian orbit, it would have developed far differently. Nevertheless it is probable that much of the Norman contribution to the English way of life only became significant because there was an Angevin 'conquest' in 1154. The Angevins were more truly French than the Normans had been in 1066, if only because in the course of that century French culture had itself became more distinctive. Under the early Angevins the attraction of the French court became so strong that England became almost a French province.

Yet England did not become part of France; and modern Frenchmen regard the English as Anglo-Saxons. One of the reasons for this later withdrawal was the very nature of the society which Norman rule had produced. The Normans in Apulia and Sicily, in England, Scotland, Ireland and the Christian Orient made their own distinctive contribution, but also assumed much of the local colour. They were a possessive race, exploiters, a true aristocracy, organizers, builders, traders, men who lived on others, greedy, but observing some restraint, careful of their lands and tenantry, respectful of local custom. Relatively unprejudiced, they were happy to lord it over any indigenous culture. Without much power of invention, they were both prepared to leave well alone and also quick to grasp the ideas of others and use them to their own advantage.

It is these qualities which make it so difficult to analyse with assurance the exact effects of the Norman conquest. The Normans neither destroyed all things English nor sank entirely into their background. Nor did they have enough time to assimilate all the ingredients and create a homogeneous structure. In 1153 the new kingdom was inchoate, diversified, inconsistent, capable of several different developments. There was increasing denationalization in the highest ranks, a growing insularity among the lesser baronage and the still largely untouched indigenous population beneath, each with its own customs. The Angevins took this strange inheritance in hand and gave it their own impression.

Select Bibliography
and Index

Select Bibliography

All works were published in London, unless otherwise stated

A. WORKS COMMON TO PARTS I, II AND IV

Sir Frank Stenton, *Anglo-Saxon England*, 2nd edn, Oxford 1947
H. R. Loyn, *Anglo-Saxon England and the Norman Conquest*, 1962
Dom D. Knowles, *The Monastic Order in England*, 2nd edn, Cambridge 1961

B. WORKS RELATING TO
PART I: THE ANGLO-SAXON ACHIEVEMENT

The Anglo-Saxon Chronicle: A Revised Translation (D. Whitelock, with D. C. Douglas and S. I. Tucker), London 1961
The Anglo-Saxon Chronicle (G. N. Garmonsway), Everyman's Library; corrected edition, 1960
D. Whitelock, *English Historical Documents*, Vol. I (*c. 500–1042*), London 1955
P. Hunter Blair, *An Introduction to Anglo-Saxon England*, Cambridge 1956
D. Whitelock, *The Beginnings of English Society* (Pelican History of England, 2), revised edition 1965
S. J. Crawford. *Anglo-Saxon Influence on Western Christendom, 600–800*, Oxford 1933
W. Levison, *England and the Continent in the Eighth Century*, Oxford 1946
J. Armitage Robinson, *The Times of St Dunstan*, Oxford 1923
R. R. Darlington, 'Ecclesiastical Reform in the Late Old English Period', *English Historical Review*, LI 1936

R. R. Darlington, *The Norman Conquest* (Creighton Lecture), 1963

F. Barlow, *The English Church, 1000–1066*, 1963

F. E. Harmer, *Anglo-Saxon Writs*, Manchester 1952

M. Dolley, *Anglo-Saxon Pennies*, British Museum 1964

G. Baldwin Brown, *The Arts in Early England*, 6 vols, 1903–37

Sir T. D. Kendrick, *Late Saxon and Viking Art*, 1948

D. M. Wilson, *The Anglo-Saxons* (Ancient Peoples and Places Series), 1960 (Chiefly archaeological)

F. Wormald, *English Drawings of the Tenth and Eleventh Centuries*, 1952

F. Wormald, *The Benedictional of St Ethelwold*, 1959

F. Wormald, 'An English Eleventh-Century Psalter with Pictures', *The Thirty-Eighth Volume of the Walpole Society*, 1960–2

M. H. Longhurst, *English Ivories*, 1926

H. M. Taylor and Joan Taylor, *Anglo-Saxon Architecture*, 2 vols, Cambridge 1965

C. WORKS RELATING TO

PART II: WILLIAM THE CONQUEROR, HIS NORMAN BACKGROUND AND ENGLISH RELATIONS

M. de Bouard, *Guillaume le Conquérant*, Paris 1958

D. C. Douglas, *William the Conqueror*, 1964

M. de Bouard, *Institutions françaises* 'Le Duché de Normandie', in F. Lot and R. Fawtier, Vol. I – Paris 1957

M. de Bouard, 'De la Neustrie carolingien à la Normandie féodale' (*Bulletin of the Inst. of Hist. Research*, XXVII, 1955)

W. J. Corbett, 'The Development of the Duchy of Normandy and the Norman Conquest of England', *Cambridge Med. Hist.*, Vol. V – 1926, Chap. XV

D. C. Douglas, 'The Rise of Normandy', British Academy *Proceedings*, Vol. XXXIII, 1947

D. C. Douglas, 'The "Song of Roland" and the Norman Conquest of England', *French Studies*, Vol. XIV, 1960

Bloch, Marc, *Feudal Society*, trans. L. A. Manyon, London 1961

C. H. Haskins, *The Normans in European History*, Cambridge, Mass. 1915

C. H. Haskins, *Norman Institutions*, Cambridge, Mass. 1918

F. Barlow, 'Edward the Confessor's Early Life, Character and Attitudes', *Eng. Hist. Rev.*, Vol. LXXX, 1965

D. C. Douglas, 'Edward the Confessor, Duke William of Normandy and the English Succession', *Eng. Hist. Rev.*, Vol. LXVIII, 1953

D. C. Douglas and G. W. Greenaway, *English Historical Documents*, Vol. II (*1042–1189*), 1953

F. Barlow, *William I and the Norman Conquest*, 1966

C. W. David, *Robert Curthose*, Harvard U.P. 1920

D. WORKS RELATING TO

PART II AND PART IV: THE NORMAN ORGANIZATION OF ENGLAND AND THE EFFECTS OF THE CONQUEST

F. Barlow, *The Feudal Kingdom of England 1042–1216*, 1961

C. W. Hollister, *Military Organisation of Norman England*, Oxford 1965

J. O. Prestwich, 'War and Finance in the Anglo Norman State' (R. Hist. Soc. *Transactions*, Series 5, Vol. IV, 1954)

Lady Stenton, *English Society in the Early Middle Ages (1066–1307)* (Pelican History of England, 3), 2nd edn, 1952

Sir Frank Stenton, *The First Century of English Feudalism*, Oxford 1961

L. C. Loyd, *The Origins of Some Anglo-Norman Families* (Harleian Society Publications, Vol. ciii, Leeds 1951)

R. L. G. Ritchie, *The Normans in Scotland*, Edinburgh 1954

Z. N. Brooke, *The English Church and the Papacy (1066–1216)*, Cambridge 1931

R. W. Southern, 'Lanfranc of Bec and Berengar of Tours', *Studies in Medieval History presented to F. M. Powicke*, 1948

F. Barlow, 'A view of Archbishop Lanfranc', *Journal of Ecclesiastical History*, 1965

R. W. Southern, *St Anselm and his Biographer*, Cambridge 1963

N. F. Cantor, *Church, Kingship and Lay Investiture in England, 1089–1135*, 1958

V. H. Galbraith, *The Making of Domesday Book*, 1961

R. Lennard, *Rural England 1086–1135*, 1959

H. G. Richardson and G. O. Sayles, *The Governance of Medieval England*, 1963

M. A. Lower, *The Chronicle of Battle Abbey (1066–c. 1190)*, 1851. (Translation of British Museum MS Cott. Dom. A. ii)

E. WORKS RELATING TO
PART III: THE CAMPAIGN OF 1066

Guillaume de Poitiers: *Gesta Guillemi Ducis . . . et Regis . . . (c.* 1073). Latin and French in parallel; translated with useful notes in French by R. Foreville, Paris 1952

E. A. Freeman, *The History of the Norman Conquest* (useful for the events before the landing in England, and for its notes), 6 vols, 1867–79

C. Dawson, *Hastings Castle*, Vol. II (for the translated passages from several Norman Chronicles), Hastings 1909

Sir Frank Stenton and others, *The Bayeux Tapestry*, 1957

Eric Maclagan, *The Bayeux Tapestry* (King Penguin) 1943

Articles on the Battle of Hastings by:

> J. F. C. Fuller (Maj.-Gen.) in *Decisive Battles of the Western World*, Vol. II, 1954
>
> A. H. Burne (Lt.-Colonel) in *The Battlefields of England*, 1951
>
> P. Young (Brig.) and J. Adair in *Hastings to Culloden*, 1964
>
> E. R. James (Maj.-Gen.) in *Royal Engineers Journal*, January 1907

C. H. Lemmon (Lt.-Colonel), *The Field of Hastings*, 3rd edn, St Leonards 1965

I. D. Margary, *Roman Ways in the Weald*, 2nd edn, 1964

C. T. Chevallier, 'Where was Malfosse', *Sussex Archaeological Collections*, Vol. 101, 1963

Hon. F. H. Baring (on William's march, Oct.–Dec. 1066) in *Notes on the Battle of Hastings*, Hastings 1906, reprinted in *Domesday Tables*, London 1909

'Viatores' (R. W. Bagshaw and others), *Roman Roads in the South East Midlands*, 1963 (for newly-traced Roman roads between London and the Ouse)

Index

Ælfric: abbot of Evesham, 19; praised tenth-century kings, 23; religious writings of, 37–8

Alcuin, scholar of York, 17, 19, 21

Aldhelm, abbot, 17, 21

Alexander II, pope: sanctions William's marriage, 61; and his invasion of England, 63, 84

Alfred, Atheling (brother of Edward the Confessor), 7, 32, 58, 62

Alfred, King: as reformer, and his successors, 15; promoter of learning and writer, 24

Angevin dynasty, 52, 53, 132; its higher French culture, 160

Anglo-Saxon: achievement, as known to Englishmen in 1050, 19–24; administration, 24–30; largely adopted by Norman kings, 70–1, 142–4; architecture, 42, 173; art, 40–1; church, 35–8, and as seen by Normans, 153–4; coinage, 29; earldoms, 30–1, 150; language, 40, 43, 137; literatue, 17, 22, 23; towns and trade, 34

Anglo-Saxon Chronicle, 10, 20, 39, 98

Anselm: archbishop of Canterbury, 156, 157; dispute over investiture, 159

Athelstan, Atheling, 5, 23

Athelstan, King, 5, 16

Battle, Sussex: strategic situation of, 95–7; site of 'Battle of Hastings', 98–9; and Battle Abbey, 3, 96, 131; see also *Senlac* for details of the battle

Bayeux Tapestry: origin of, 11, 41; cited, 78, 84, 85, 86, 89, 107, 152

Bede, Venerable, historian and theologian, 15, 17, 19, 21, 38

Beorn, earl of Hereford, 9, 32

Beowulf, 18

Boniface, St (of Crediton), bishop of Mainz, 15, 17, 21

Bow, short, range of, 105

Brunanburh, battle of, 16, 20

Byrhtnoth: in *Song of Maldon*, 22, 39; tapestry commemorating, 12

Church: Anglo-Norman, 67–9; as pacifying influence, 130–1; high offices filled by Normans, 68, 132; reorganized by